For my sister-in-law Anna Baldwin, a real mediaeval scholar,
with love — M.H.

For my precious Poppie and Kiki and our beloved 'Shaman' — C.B.

First published in the United States of America in 2000 by Abbeville Press,
22 Cortlandt Street, New York, N.Y. 10007
Women of Camelot copyright © Frances Lincoln Limited 2000
Text copyright © Mary Hoffman 2000
Illustrations copyright © Christina Balit 2000

First published in Great Britain in 2000 by
Frances Lincoln Limited

Printed and bound in Hong Kong.
First Edition

1 3 5 7 9 10 8 6 4 2

Library of Congress Cataloging-in-Publication Data

Hoffman, Mary, 1945-
Women of Camelot : queens and enchantresses at the court of King Arthur / Mary
Hoffman ; illustrated by Christina Balit.
P. Cm.
Summary: Women characters from Arthurian legends, including Guinevere, Igrayne,
and Elaine, tell their stories.
ISBN 0-7892-0646-3(alk.paper)
1. Arthur, King—Juvenile fiction. [1. Arthur, King—Fiction. 2. Knights and
knighthood—Fiction. 3. England—Fiction.] I. Balit, Christina, ill. II. Title.
PZ7.H67562 Wo 2000
[Fic]—dc21
00-086627

ISBN 0-7892-0646-3

WOMEN OF CAMELOT

QUEENS AND ENCHANTRESSES AT THE COURT OF KING ARTHUR

MARY HOFFMAN
Illustrated by CHRISTINA BALIT

Abbeville Press Publishers
New York London Paris

KING ARTHUR'S FAMILY TREE

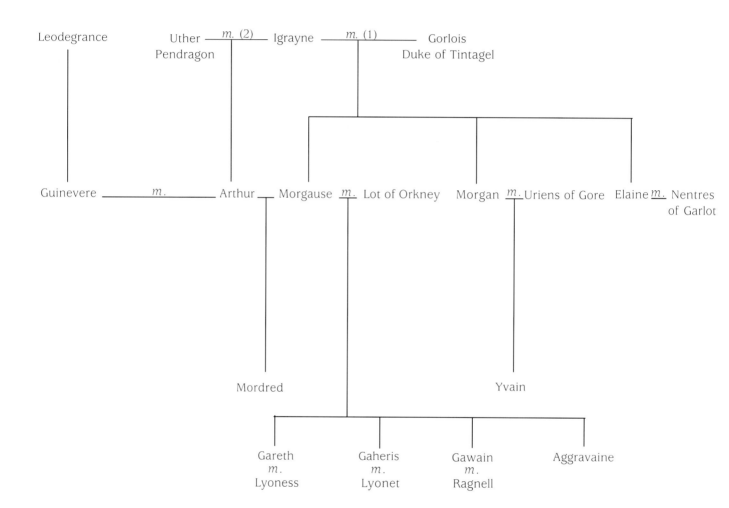

Leodegrance   Uther —— *m.* (2) —— Igrayne —— *m.* (1) —— Gorlois
        Pendragon   Duke of Tintagel

Guinevere —— *m.* —— Arthur —— Morgause *m.* Lot of Orkney   Morgan *m.* Uriens of Gore   Elaine *m.* Nentres
                                                                  of Garlot

Mordred   Yvain

Gareth   Gaheris   Gawain   Aggravaine
m.   *m.*   *m.*
Lyoness   Lyonet   Ragnell

CONTENTS

INTRODUCTION

If you have heard the name Camelot, it may conjure up knights in shining armor, riding off to rescue damsels in distress or to joust in tournaments, wearing a lady's token in their helmets. This was an important part of the life of King Arthur's knights of the Round Table, but you won't find many of those stories here. Instead, you will read about the women, the ones who were left behind when the men went out on quests and adventures.

But these weren't just stay-at-homes. They were influential queens and powerful sorceresses, and even ordinary women who were determined and resourceful. In spite of the restrictions of their lives, the women often lie at the heart of the stories and, by one means or another, they make things happen ...

MOTHER *of* MAGIC: IGRAYNE'S STORY

This is the story of the woman who became mother to Arthur, the most famous king England ever had. But she also had three daughters, and they made their glorious half brother's life as difficult as possible.

I never thought of myself as beautiful. When I was a girl, all those long years ago in Wales, my mother thought I was a terrible rebel, and I never cared about how I looked. When I was little, I often wouldn't stand still long enough for my hair to be brushed, let alone braided. Strange to think I now wear the stiff gowns and heavy jewels of a queen, and the hours hang heavy on my hands. Back then the days just weren't long enough for all I wanted to do. There were dogs to run with, horses to ride, fields and woods to explore.

But those wild days came to an end when my mother told me that I was nearly a woman and must learn how to sit still, to smile, and to sing. My father said I would never get a husband by running in the woods, and so he gave me a harp and a tapestry frame. I didn't mind the singing; my teacher was a young troubadour with a lovely smile of his own. But how I hated that tapestry!

The days were long indeed as I sat making knots in my thread and pricking my clumsy fingers. My younger sisters had no such duties and chores. And the evenings were even longer when I had to serve the visitors at my hospitable father's table in the Hall, wearing an awkward long-sleeved dress, instead of taking my meat with my brothers and sisters in the winter parlor.

The best part was when everyone had eaten their fill, and I could slip behind a pillar and listen to Rhodri the handsome troubadour playing his harp and singing of Bran the Blessed or Rhiannon the witch. According to Father, we can trace our ancestors back to Bran — which gives me a strange feeling when I hear the stories that are told about him, how his head talked after it was cut off, and how he never died but will come back to save Britain in its hour of need.

It was on one of those evenings that I first saw my husband — my real

husband, the one I loved. It was he who made me realize I was beautiful. Our visitor never took his eyes from me all that first evening, and I became confused and clumsy, splashing tunics with wine and dropping a platter. In the end my father sent me out of the Hall and I buried my face, burning with embarrassment, in my pillow and went to sleep without any supper.

It didn't take me long to find out that this lord was the Duke of Cornwall and that his name was Gorlois. And he wasted no time in finding out my name, too. Almost as soon as he knew it, he asked my father to give me to him for a wife. We hadn't exchanged more than half a dozen words before I was on my way to Cornwall with him as my husband, leaving my family behind in Wales.

It was all so sudden. What did I know of being a wife and running a noble household? I was barely sixteen, as ignorant and innocent as a Welsh hill sheep. But Gorlois didn't mind. When he brought me into his castle at Tintagel, on a Cornish coast as wild as any in my home country, he gathered me in his arms and, smiling, taught me all I needed to know.

He was older than me by about ten years and had a smoothly running household already. "What do you need a wife for?" I used to tease him, lying in his arms all that first long summer, and he would tease me back, "Just for ornament, my beauty." How happy we were! I would not have thought it possible to be any happier, but by the next spring we had our first little girl, Morgause, and we were even more in love.

Gorlois never minded not having a son, never showed a moment's disappointment when Elaine and Morgan were born in the years that followed. "Let Cornwall have a duchess!" he'd say. "Morgause is a good enough heir for me." But I wanted to give him a son and perhaps I would have, if it hadn't been for my accursed face.

I blame Rhodri, the troubadour, who left my father's house and eventually entered the king's service. I didn't know it then, but I found out later that he had made up a ballad about me, called "The Fair Maid of Wales." He sang my praises, literally, at the court of King Uther, until the mighty king himself asked Rhodri what had become of me.

It was silly, of course. I wasn't a maid anymore, but a wife and mother; as for fair, was I the only good-looking woman in the country? I don't deny that I was beautiful. Gorlois told me I was, and so had Rhodri during our harp lessons when I was a girl. But I wasn't vain about my looks. If I could have kept my true love and the life we had those first few years at Tintagel, I would gladly have given up a pleasing face and pretty figure, things which time would have stolen in due course, anyway.

I was looking out of a window when the messenger rode across our narrow bridge. My blood seemed to stop its journey through my body when I saw the insignia of Uther Pendragon. That's the second sight. All the women in our family have it; some more than others.

My mother had been at Tintagel for the birth of all my daughters and Elaine was the only one she had no word of prophecy about. When firstly Morgause was born, after a long hard time of it, my mother held her and said, "Her sons will be greater than their father, all except the last," and, "She will be a thorn in her brother's side." But when she held newborn Morgan, she almost dropped her. "This one has more power in her than the rest of us put together," she said, then quickly forgot what she had seen.

She was always like that, having visions and then being unable to remember them. But I never forgot what she said about Morgause's brother. That's why I always thought Gorlois and I would have a son. Remembering Mother's other prediction, I decided to put Morgan in a convent as soon as she was old enough.

The day the messenger came, I knew my intuition hadn't played any tricks. Gorlois was entertaining Uther's courtier in the Great Hall.

"My Lady," said Gorlois, "we are honored indeed. The king has sent a most gracious invitation that we should both attend him at his court."

I was silent throughout the meal, but my mind was racing. Morgause and Elaine were old enough to leave behind, since they were teenagers, but Morgan was still a baby. I was still nursing her, so I could not travel to London without her. But when I spoke to Gorlois alone, he brushed all my objections aside.

"It would be madness to refuse an invitation from the king himself," he said.

"But the baby," I protested. "I don't want to leave her!"

"Then we'll take her with us," he smiled, gathering me into his arms. "I am sure King Uther won't mind. And before you say anything about the other two, there are women enough at Tintagel to look after them until we return."

We left our castle on a summer morning, riding our horses over the high bridge, but once over, I was carried the rest of the weary way on a raised seat with my baby. She fussed and fretted for most of the journey, and as we entered the king's palace, she began to wail.

I could still hear her when I left her in our chamber with my waiting-woman and went down to meet the king. I took little trouble with my hair and dress at first, but Gorlois made me do it all again. It was the only time in all our happy marriage that he was angry with me. He said I must wear the richest gown and my most precious jewels, or I would shame him before the king.

I knew as soon as Uther looked in my face that he had made up his mind to have me. I have heard the rumor in later years, that I had

bewitched him, but it is not true. He bewitched himself. He fell in love with a woman in a song, and sadly for me, I was that lady.

I tried to tell Gorlois my fears. "Please let us go back to Tintagel," I begged. "I know that evil will come of this visit."

Gorlois was used to the women in my family having an extra sense about such things.

"My darling," he said, stroking my hair, "I have seen the way the king looks at you, and I think you may be right. I will protect you from him with my life, but I cannot risk offending him by leaving without a reason."

We soon had a reason. Uther sent a golden cup to my chamber, bidding me to drink my wine from it. Soon afterwards, when I was alone, he came himself. I remember nothing of what he said, only that Morgan, who was in her crib, stopped her wailing when he came into the room. I would have said she was studying his face, as if to remember him.

When I showed Gorlois the cup and told him of the king's secret visit, he agreed that we must leave with all haste. How happily I rode out from that hateful palace! My heart grew lighter with every pace the horses took towards Cornwall.

But my joy was short-lived. Within a few hours of our return, a message came to say that Uther was pursuing us from London. He was very angry that we had left without permission.

As soon as we reached Tintagel, Gorlois raised his men and set out to fortify his other castle, a few miles away at Damelioc, that the locals called Castle Terrible. And it was terrible indeed for us. I saw my husband only once more. Uther sent a great army, far more soldiers than a duke could command. I stayed confined in Tintagel, hardly sleeping, not daring to believe that my beloved could overcome a king.

So imagine my delight when one night I heard horses' hooves on the narrow bridge. I ran to the window. It was my lord! We had been apart so long that we fell into each other's arms with no thought of anyone else. We spoke little that night. Gorlois stole away from our bedroom before daybreak to go back to Castle Terrible — or so I thought.

But at dawn there came a messenger to say that Gorlois was dead; my lord and love had been killed in a surprise attack by Uther's men. That was tragedy enough, but the messenger went on to say that my husband had died the night before — three hours before Gorlois came to my bed!

I think I must have lost my mind for some days after that. Only the thought of our daughters stopped me from jumping from the battlements onto the rocks below. I know my waiting-women thought I might kill myself, for they watched me every hour.

As the days went by, I found another reason to live. I knew the signs well enough by now, and I was sure that this time I would bear a son. Foolishly I reasoned that Gorlois must have visited me as a phantom, spurred on by a love greater than death.

And yet I listened to King Uther's proposals of marriage. Most women would think I was a traitor. I was not. My daughters and the child that was coming needed the protection of a father. Uther had already promised to find kings to marry my older girls, though he agreed to my request that Morgan should become a holy sister. And I thought that if I married Uther, Gorlois would not have died in vain. He and many brave men had given their lives because the king wanted me for himself. Marriage to Uther, whom I didn't love, would be my punishment for the deaths of those knights. But I would never forget Gorlois, my first and only love.

So King Uther and I were wed, and I became Queen of Logres. Never again would I know the happiness of the Welsh rebel running through the fields, nor of the Cornish duchess playing house in her husband's castle. Now I wore a gold crown and had servants to obey my slightest wish.

Only once did I regret my decision, and that was the night Uther told me he was the father of my growing child. He had a counselor at his court named Merlin, a great master of the dark arts. It was Merlin who had disguised the king as Gorlois, that last night I thought I held him in my arms. It was a bitter truth to swallow, but my second sight recognized it was true.

Uther had the baby taken away as soon as it was born. Perhaps it was just as well. It was a boy, a fine, healthy, energetically yelling one, but I had no desire to hold him or nurse him. I turned aside as Uther gave the child, all swaddled up, to Merlin. The king had agreed earlier to give the child to Merlin, in return for his help in disguising him that night in Tintagel.

Little did I think that I would ever see my son again, much less that he would be King Arthur, the High King of Logres!

And God was good to me, for within two years King Uther was dead, and I was allowed to go and live with my eldest daughter, who was now a queen herself in Scotland.

I have lived for many years in the wild kingdom of Orkney, enjoying my many grandsons, living in great comfort and remembering my Gorlois. But, as for my son the king, you must hear of him from others ...

QUEEN *of the* ROUND TABLE: GUINEVERE'S STORY

Igrayne's son Arthur became king of England in a miraculous fashion. He was brought up by Sir Ector's wife and believed himself to be Sir Ector's son. One New Year's Day, Sir Ector brought Arthur and his older son Sir Kay to London for a tournament. Kay was a participant but had left his sword behind at the inn. As the youngest, Arthur was sent to fetch the sword. But he found no one at home to give it to him because they were all at the tournament.

Arthur didn't want to go back empty-handed, so he wandered around London until he found himself by a churchyard. There stood a strange sight: a huge rock with an anvil embedded in it, and into the anvil had been thrust a sword. Arthur did not stop to read the inscription on the stone. He was so happy to have found a sword for Kay that he quickly pulled it out of the anvil and hurried back to the tournament.

Sir Ector recognized the sword right away. Its miraculous appearance in the churchyard years ago had been the talk of the kingdom. And Sir Ector remembered what the inscription had said. He took Kay and Arthur to read it:

> *WHOEVER PULLS THE SWORD OUT OF THIS STONE AND ANVIL IS THE RIGHTFUL KING OF ALL ENGLAND.*

Sir Ector made Arthur put the sword back in and draw it out again, which he did — as easily as taking a knife from butter. Many knights had tried to pull it out before and it had not shifted an inch. Now a mere boy had done what all the best knights in the land had failed to do. Sir Ector and Sir Kay knelt at Arthur's feet. They were the first to recognize him as the true king of England.

At Pentecost a great feast was held, at which many nobles accepted Arthur as their king. But others were harder to convince. Merlin told how Arthur had been conceived by Queen Ingrayne and King Uther in the likeness of Duke Gorlois, and how the king had married Igrayne soon after, and Arthur had been removed to Sir Ector's house as soon as he was born.

There were eleven kings of small countries in the British Isles, including Lot of Orkney, Uriens of Gore and Nentres of Garlot, who didn't believe the story. They waged war on the young King Arthur, thinking it would be easy to overthrow a beardless boy and his strange counselor, Merlin.

Arthur and his band of young followers defeated the rebel kings in a great battle. But Uriens continued to be a problem. He surrounded King Leodegrance's castle at Camelard, and Arthur came to the rescue. It was there that the young king first caught sight of a woman called Guinevere ...

There is nothing more boring than to be surrounded by an enemy's army! You cannot leave the castle walls, find any fresh food to eat, or breathe any fresh air. Everyone is tense, but fear soon gives way to boredom after days and weeks of inaction. But there came a day when there was certainly action enough. A troop of King Uriens' men breached the wall, broke into the castle, and kidnapped my father!

It all happened so suddenly that our men were helpless. But not as helpless as I felt, and I needed all my confidence and authority to prevent our people from giving way to despair. I tried to keep the soldiers' spirits up, but in my heart I had no idea what we should do. I thought my first and last act as warrior princess would be to surrender the castle.

But one night, a strange visitor came to the gate. No one knew how he had slipped past the besieging army. He was unarmed except for a staff, so I allowed him to come in. He did not give his name, but that is not uncommon, and it is discourteous to pry when great men walk the land in disguise. I had no doubt that he was a great man, because his torn and dusty clothes showed that he had endured much.

The stranger was neither young nor old, short nor tall. But he was handsome and well-spoken, and he had the strangest black eyes, very deep set, with hooded lids. There was something about him not quite of this world.

"Princess," he said, "forgive my intrusion. I come with news of your father. King Leodegrance is safe. It was my privilege to rescue him from the rebels."

"Jesus be praised!" I replied. "And all praise to you, kind stranger, for your good deed. But where is the king? And how may we repay you?"

"He is nearby, in the safe custody of my young master. And as for repayment, do not speak of it. I only ask that my lord and I, and our following of fighting men, should have the privilege of serving you. May we seek food and shelter within your walls?"

This strange man seemed to have been sent by a higher power. We housed and fed him with great honor, as well as we could with only salt meat and twice-baked bread, and the next morning he departed. But he was back by nightfall with my father, the young man he called lord and a mighty company of men on horseback.

They had to cut their way to the gates through the rebel army, and some of the men were wounded. My father was a changed man after the long idleness of the siege. He swept through the castle, gave me a quick kiss on the cheek, and ordered the waiting-women to care for the wounded and find stables and feed for the horses.

At our meager supper that night, served on the best gold plates, my father

bade me to take wine to the young lord and the dark-eyed stranger who seemed to be his adviser. I lowered my eyes, as is our custom, but couldn't resist looking upward when the young lord drank. I felt a deep flush rising from my throat to my face.

He was not as fascinating to look at as his counselor, and there was nothing otherworldly about him. But he had such vigor, and he wore authority like a cloak. He would not tell my father his name, but somehow I knew he was a king. In the early stages of the siege, I had heard a rumor from my waiting-women that my father might marry me off to old King Uriens. Now, looking at this stranger, I knew that he would make a very different kind of husband.

Our deliverers lost no time in giving battle to the rebel king. Within a short time Uriens and his forces had been routed and we were roasting freshly-killed oxen for a victory banquet.

I had been self-conscious enough when I first served wine to our unknown guests. But it was even worse after their great triumph. I overheard the young lord speaking to Leodegrance about marrying me. Now, my father didn't have to ask my opinion, even though I had never exchanged a word with the young man. Daughters of kings are married for political reasons, not love, and I had been brought up to believe I would be a queen.

But my father did glance towards me, and I did give the smallest nod. Not so small that the golden hero didn't see it, though. He looked straight towards me and smiled, a smile that caused my hands to falter and the wine to spill on my white gown. It looked like a blood stain, and for a moment my heart stopped, too. Was it an omen? What did we know about this man? Perhaps I was making a terrible mistake.

But my misgivings were soon forgotten when our visitors revealed who they were. Arthur, king of all Logres, was to be my wedded lord! And his counselor was Merlin, feared and respected in equal measure, a man rumored to be a wizard and to practice black magic.

The next Whitsunday, Arthur and I were married and crowned at Caerleon with great ceremony. Four queens walked into the church before me, each carrying a white dove. They were Arthur's noble mother Igrayne and her three daughters by her first marriage.

Igrayne accepted me most graciously and the middle sister, Elaine, was a sweet, loving girl, but Arthur's other two half sisters were a different matter. They were all queens by virtue of their marriages. Elaine's husband was Nentres of Garlot. Morgause had been married for some years to the king of Orkney and had a brood of boisterous sons. She herself was a handsome woman in a big and blowsy style, like an overripe peach, and she looked at me in the oddest way, as if she knew secrets that I didn't.

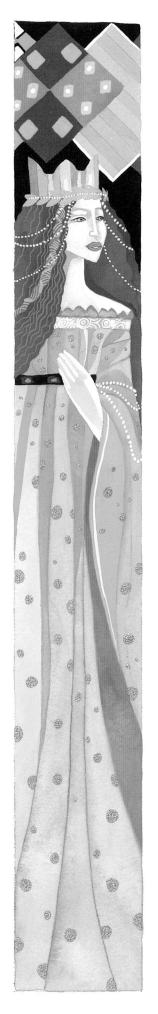

And the youngest, Morgan, had been hastily married off to Uriens the month before, to strengthen his allegiance to Arthur.

At first I thought Morgan was jealous of me for marrying a handsome young king while she had a husband so much older. But later I realized that her ill will was aimed at my husband and not at me. And I felt, from the moment I met her, that she could be a deadly opponent.

Which woman doesn't carry family secrets and feuds in her heart on her wedding day? But I was determined to behave like a queen. My entire life had been a preparation for this day. And, drawn though I was to the young king, in my mind it was not our marriage but the coronation that was the more solemn ceremony.

I wore a dress of green silk sprinkled with emeralds, and I was crowned with laurel. The archbishop anointed my hands and cheeks and hair, which meant no mortal but my husband could ever again touch me in those places. Nor must I ever touch base metals, such as iron or bronze — only gold, silver and copper may touch my skin. And I had to swear never to cut my hair or to let blood intentionally.

The celebrations and feasting went on for days. My father gave us a strange wedding present: a huge round table which had come from Arthur's father, Uther Pendragon. My new husband was extremely excited about this part of my dowry and seemed to think more of it than all my lands. He had the table set up in his banqueting hall in Camelot, and there were places for one hundred and fifty to sit at it. In every seat there magically appeared, written in gold letters, the name of the knight who sat in it, as he took his place. All except one — that of the Siege Perilous, the dangerous seat, which was reserved for the best knight in the world.

But at the time of our marriage, Arthur had scarcely thirty knights to sit at the Round Table, and from then on he dedicated himself to filling all the seats with the best English men. He wanted brave young men devoted to righting wrongs and protecting the innocent, especially women. There was no place for women to sit at that table, though I, a woman, had brought it to Arthur's court. But I was proud, too, as the seats filled up and the fellowship's reputation for chivalry grew.

And at first I was happy in my marriage. The king my husband never lost for me that air of someone above other mortal men. Time and again I saw new knights won over to him and ready to dedicate their whole lives to his service. Arthur was that kind of man: people would swear loyalty to him to their lives' end. And for a long time I felt the same.

It was Arthur's sister, Queen Morgan, who planted the first seeds of doubt in my mind. She was visiting with Uriens and her small son Yvain. I had just lost my first child at a very early stage and was feeling sad and bitterly disappointed. But queens do not weep, and I entertained Morgan royally and politely. She did not respond in like manner.

"See what a vigorous heir my old husband has," she said, speaking of Uriens as I never would have done, and admiring her little boy playing at our feet. I lifted him onto my lap and stroked his dark curls. The sweet child cooed and smiled.

"You are indeed most fortunate," I said formally, as my empty womb ached for a boy of my own.

"We Cornish women are a fertile race," Morgan went on, looking sideways at me. "Look at my eldest sister Morgause. King Lot has four heirs to carry on his line."

"I believe your sister has five sons," I said. "I trust nothing has happened to any of them."

"No, they are all well, praise God," said Morgan. "But no thanks to Arthur. You know he had all the children of noble birth who were born last May Day drowned?"

I could hardly believe such a thing of my lord, so I said nothing.

"My youngest nephew, Mordred, was one of the unfortunates," continued Morgan, taking Yvain from me and rocking him in her own lap. "But fate intervened. He was rescued and is thriving."

She looked at me with her dark witch's eyes, expecting more questions, and I couldn't help myself.

"Then King Lot still has five heirs?"

Morgan snorted. "You must ask your husband about that," she said. "Do you think he would have been interested in killing Lot's children? No, Morgause had swerved from Lot's bed when she conceived her youngest son."

I felt myself blushing. This was no way for Morgan to speak of her sister; and she a crowned queen, too! I marveled that Morgan had no shame. And even if such a scandalous thing were true, what could it have to do with my husband?

"Ask him," said Morgan, as if reading my thoughts. "And ask him also about the Round Table."

"What of it?" I asked, pretending to laugh. I could see nothing sinister in a piece of furniture.

"Ask which he needed more," said Morgan, "a wife, or something of King Uther's."

At that, I rose hastily and left the room.

That night, as I sat combing my hair before the great mirror Arthur had given to me, I told him about my conversation with his half sister, expecting him to laugh it off as part of Morgan's usual mischief-making. But instead

he told me something that changed our lives forever. He said that Mordred, Morgause's youngest child, was his own son! The lecherous queen had come to Arthur's court when he first claimed the crown, and her great beauty had seduced him into bed with her. He hadn't known at that time that he was related to her, and it was Merlin who later told him the shameful truth, that he and Morgause shared the same mother. Then Merlin prophesied that Mordred would bring great ruin on Arthur's kingdom, and to prevent such a fate was the reason why Arthur had given his cruel command concerning the May Day babies.

I never felt the same about Arthur after that. Nor did I ever ask him about the Round Table. The revelations about Mordred had driven that out of my mind. And I realized that if Arthur had already fathered a son, it was my fault that he had not yet had an heir by me. And much later I remembered Morgan's words. Had Arthur needed a wife, or something of Uther's?

And I remembered the fuss Arthur had made about that wretched table. Uther Pendragon had given it to my father — but now that Arthur had the table, it helped to prove to all the doubters that he was Uther's son. They had heard the story of his conception, but a table is a more solid piece of evidence than a tale of a false adoption. In time, the common people would forget how Arthur acquired it and see it as a legacy from his father.

It was then I realized that my husband was more the politician than the lover, and that his reasons for marrying me were no more sentimental than old King Uriens' would have been. From that moment, I doubted that Arthur had ever loved me, and it wounded me to the quick. I was determined to fulfill my role as his queen, however, and to give him an heir if I could. But my heart turned away from him and a distance grew between us.

MERLIN'S BANE: NIMUE'S STORY

The life of King Arthur was crisscrossed with miraculous events. People might not be what they seemed, and scenes could change in the flicker of an eye from the mundane to the magical. And no one knew this better than Arthur's wise counselor, Merlin, or his pupil, Nimue ...

He fascinated me from our first meeting: Merlin, born of the devil and a mortal woman so pious that the evil in him was canceled out. It left him wise and powerful, able to do what no other man could but always dangerous and unpredictable.

I didn't know who he was when I first met him. I was only twelve. My father lived in a castle given to him by King Ban of Benwick, and it was set in a fair countryside. There was a fountain in the grounds that bubbled up from a natural source and flowed over its stony bed, so pure that you could see every grain and pebble through its clear water. I used to sit by the fountain for hours, trailing my fingers through the cold water and dreaming of my future.

One day I looked up and there he was: a young man with old eyes, yet handsome enough by worldly standards, with his straight back and glossy black hair, but with something else about him, too. Before he even spoke, I sensed the magic in him. The only feeling I can compare it to is the taste in the air when a thunderstorm is coming, and the cats race around the barn.

We had such a strange conversation. He told me about his teacher, Blaise.

"My master taught me how to raise a castle up into the air, so that you can see the sun shining underneath it," he said.

"Really?" I said, my eyes shining. "Could you do that to my castle?"

But he didn't.

"I can walk through that brook and remain dry," he said, and with a little persuasion he did. I felt his shoes and they were as dry as the day they were made.

And when he told me that he could flood a dry plain with water, conjuring it out of nowhere, I believed him.

I was bewitched. I don't mean that Merlin cast a spell on me, unless it is magic that makes a woman love a man. He charmed me with his strange personality and the things he talked about. He made me want to learn the things that he could do — and do them myself.

"Are you a scholar?" he asked, though he could see I was just a little girl. "Would you like me to teach you the magic arts?"

From that moment I was lost. By the time Merlin left that shady glade and before I even knew his name, we were betrothed. He solemnly drew a circle round me on the grass, a small circle to enclose and protect me while he was away. How proud I was! But in time that magic circle became a weary prison.

I ran home to the castle lightheartedly and told my father, Dionas, that I had met an extraordinary man, and that when I grew up I was going to spend the rest of my life with him. My father took it very well.

"I've been expecting this," he said, "from the day you were born. Before you were even conceived, there was a prophecy that you would marry Merlin."

Merlin. That was the first time I heard his name. My father told me that many people feared my mysterious suitor. Some called him demon, some wizard, but all were agreed he was a dangerous man to cross. What did I care? My heart sang like the blackbird my beloved took his name from. I knew that Merlin would be my tame blackbird and never bite the hand of his mistress.

The first real magic Merlin taught me was how to flood water over dry land. It was an illusion, of course, and at first it hurt every nerve in my body to create it. But the water seemed real enough to drink and to be able to drown a man as effectively as a real flood. It gradually became easier to do, and soon I could summon water out of the air without a twinge of discomfort.

Water became my trademark. People began to call me the Lady of the Lake, even while I was still a young maid. My father wouldn't let me live with Merlin until I was fifteen, but in those three years my beloved wizard taught me every day, except when he was away at the court of King Ban or King Arthur. He was a hard taskmaster and kept me at my books ten hours a day. But I didn't mind. I loved to study.

As Merlin's knowledge passed from him to me, he seemed to grow more in love and I less so. The more I understood how he did things, the less fascinating I found him. It was cruel of me to feel that way, and now and then I would be overcome with a rush of pity and affection for him that was almost as good as love. Yet always I felt the shape of that circle around me, marking me out as his property, and it irked me more with every year that passed.

When I was fifteen and left my home, I gained a new sense of freedom. I traveled with Merlin to the court of King Ban, and that is where I found the true love of my life. The king's wife had just had a baby son and Ban proudly showed him off to us. That was my first sight of Lancelot. I never bore a child myself, but no woman could ever love a son more than I came to love that boy.

Within twelve months of first seeing Lancelot, I became his foster mother. It happened like this. King Ban was mercilessly killed by his enemy King Claudas while Ban was out on the mountainside with his wife and little son. The queen ran, distraught, up the mountain in search of her husband, leaving her baby lying on the grass.

But Lancelot was a vigorous child. He tried to push himself up on his elbows and began to roll down the mountainside. Fortunately I was nearby, and so strong was my connection to the infant Lancelot that I sensed that he was in danger. In an instant I created a lake at the foot of the mountain, and instead of being dashed to death on the rocks, the boy fell down the bank and into its gentle waters.

I took him up in my arms and kept him in my care until he was eighteen years old. I brought him up in ignorance of his name. I called him Fitzroy, ("king's son"), and I gave him a garland of white roses every day of his life, for by then I was a skilled enough scholar ("enchantress," as the local people preferred to put it) to be able to do that.

It was Merlin who turned my attention to Camelot. He told me that the whole future of Logres depended on keeping Arthur on the throne, and Merlin needed my help to do it. We spent long hours forging the sword Excalibur, surrounding every stage of its making with what the ignorant folk call spells. I wove the scabbard myself and stitched in all the pierced gems that encrusted it. The scabbard was worth even more than the sword, for woven into it was a spell which protected the wearer against all injury.

I had my own lake by now, a real one in front of my own castle. Merlin brought Arthur there after he lost his first sword, the one he pulled out of the stone. I made Excalibur rise out of the water, making it appear in the hand of a woman clothed in white silk. Then I used one of the early skills Merlin had taught me. I walked across the lake and brought the sword to Arthur.

I wonder what the great king would have thought if he had known that I had in my castle a boy destined to be the greatest knight of the Round Table and Arthur's best friend — and yet the man whose actions would bring the whole fellowship to ruin.

Merlin advised Arthur for some years. He even warned him about marrying Guinevere. Someone should have warned Merlin about staying with me. In our early years I was so much under his spell that I feared his power. So I made him swear that he would never use enchantment against me and that he would teach me anything I asked to learn.

He loved me so much that he agreed. Poor man! For he *was*

a man, and not a fiend, as so many people imagined. And he taught me the two things I most needed to know: how to draw the magic circle and how to unmake it. He looked at me through black eyes heavy with years of learning in his smooth brown face, and I saw that he knew what I was going to do. But he told me, anyway.

We were walking in the forest of Broceliande, near my childhood home. It was May and the sun was warm. After Merlin told me what I needed to know, he became drowsy. We sat and rested under a hawthorn tree, and he laid his head in my lap. As soon as he was asleep, I kissed his eyes and gently eased myself from underneath him.

It took hours, first to draw a circle strong enough to bind the world's greatest enchanter, then to draw a bigger one enclosing the whole tree, so that no one should ever find him. It helped that it was a hawthorn tree, heavy with scent and with magical properties of its own. Finally, I had to unmake the circle he had drawn round me all those years ago when I was a child yearning for magic.

It was the hardest thing I had ever done. When it was over, I was exhausted. People say that I killed Merlin or buried him alive, but I would never have hurt him. I just needed to be freed from him.

I still go and visit him in Broceliande, where his hawthorn tree is always in bloom, suspended in time. He is there still, waiting for someone to unmake the circle that holds him. He cannot do it himself: I had to take his powers away while he slept in order to summon enough energy to draw his circle and unmake mine.

Over the years those powers have become almost too much for me. It is like wrestling with a serpent every day. I am free of Merlin, but he is still with me. So I shall go to the Grail Castle. There is a goodness in it that I need. If I can see the holy cup and be visited by God's grace, I may be given the strength to control the magic within me. I cannot forget that Merlin's father was supposed to have been a demon. He was so full of goodness himself that he tamed his inheritance, but I was little more than a girl when I took all his power on myself.

It has been a heavy burden. All I seek now is peace.

THE SAVAGE DAMSEL: LYONET'S STORY

*As the years passed, the fellowship of the Round Table grew in fame.
Sir Gawain, Sir Tristram, and Sir Lancelot were renowned for their
strength in combat and their chivalrous behavior. Arthur made all his knights
swear to protect every woman who needed a hero and serve them
with their strength in arms. Lyonet is one such damsel who came to
Arthur's castle at Caerleon seeking help. She chose Whitsunday, knowing
that the King would never sit down to his dinner on a High Feast Day
until some adventure presented itself.*

needed a hero. And where else should I find one but at the court of King Arthur? It was actually my sister, the Lady Lyoness, who needed a champion. She had been kept a prisoner in her castle by a violent lord known as the Red Knight of the Red Lands. He had no claim on her property, and she was desperate to be saved from him.

So I set off to see these fine knights of the Round Table and try to persuade one of the famous ones to come and defend Lyoness. I timed my journey well, so that I should arrive at King Arthur's castle in Caerleon on Whitsunday.

I entered King Arthur's Hall, my heart pounding, but I held my head up high. Then I curtseyed to him, scarcely seeing Queen Guinevere or any of the other fine people sitting at the King's table.

"Sire," I said, "my sister is a noble lady and her lands are being besieged by a tyrant. She cannot leave her own castle. I have come to you for help, because it is said this is the noblest fellowship of knights in the world."

"Who is your sister?" asked the king kindly. "And who is it that besieges her?"

"I may not tell you her name at this time," I said, as Lyoness had instructed me, "but the tyrant is the Red Knight of the Red Lands."

"Fair damsel," said King Arthur, "my court is full of knights who would rescue your sister, but if you will not reveal her name, I cannot grant them this adventure."

I was in a dilemma; I couldn't go back to my sister without a hero. Then matters went from bad to worse. A tall, lean young man, wearing — I swear it! — an apron, came forward.

"I have been at your court a year, my liege," he said to the king, "and you have given me food and drink as I asked. Now it is time to grant me my

other two requests."

Everyone in the court was looking at this adolescent youth and seemed to have forgotten all about me.

"Grant me this adventure of the lady in the castle," said the young man. "And let Sir Lancelot make me a knight before I set out."

This presumptuous young man wasn't even a knight! He seemed to be some sort of kitchen hand. I thought King Arthur would laugh in his face. But the king took him seriously and said, "It shall be as you ask."

I could hardly tell the High King that I thought he had taken leave of his senses, so I did the next best thing: I flounced out.

I was riding back to Castle Dangerous when I heard hoofbeats behind me. I turned to see if one of the great knights had taken pity on me, but no, it was the kitchen boy. However, he had a good horse, and he looked well enough in his armor, and his saddle and bridle were decorated in gold, just as if he had been a man of quality.

After him rode a real hero, Sir Lancelot — an altogether more impressive figure. I kept out of earshot, but I watched them eagerly debating, and I believe that the kitchen hand might have told Sir Lancelot some secret he didn't want me to hear. I saw the boy fall to his knees, and Lancelot took his own sword and tapped the mighty blade lightly on each shoulder. I wondered what he said then: Arise, Sir Drudge?

As soon as the deed was done, Sir Lancelot rode back to the court.

So now I had a champion and a knight, but not the one I wanted, so I wasn't about to make this one's life easy.

"If you must follow me, idler," I said, "keep well behind. You stink of the kitchen, and you are covered with grease and lard. You are unworthy to ride so close to a gentlewoman."

Although he was so big and strong, I thought he would be of no use to me unless I could get him fired up. But he was very unsatisfying to scold and seemed not to care what I said.

"You will need all your courage," I warned him, "for you will have to do battle with a knight you wouldn't want to face despite all the soup you have ever stirred."

"Well," said my knight of the kitchen, "I have sworn to carry out this adventure, so I will endure it to the end, whatever you say."

We rode on until evening and came to the Black Lands. There, by a black hawthorn tree, sat a knight in black armor on a black horse.

"Ha, is this the champion you have brought back from King Arthur's court?" he asked.

"No," I replied. "This is the king's kitchen boy, who has been getting free dinners this last year. He insisted on following me."

"Hmm," said the Black Knight. "He looks strong enough, even though he is no gentleman. And he has a fine horse and harness, which I will take from him."

"You will have to win it first," said the kitchen knight calmly, "and I am as much of a gentleman as you are, so show me what you can do."

They jousted together with spear and sword. I couldn't bear to watch, so I rode on. Soon I heard a horseman behind me, and turned and saw a knight in black armor on a black horse. So much for my hero! But imagine my surprise when he raised his helmet's visor, and I saw it was the kitchen knight!

"I have killed the Black Knight," he said calmly, "and have taken his horse and armor, since he would have done the same to me."

"What a pity!" I said, though I was shaking all over. "For he was of good birth and didn't deserve to be killed by a kitchen knight. Still, he will soon be avenged, for he has many brave brothers between here and Castle Dangerous."

And this was true enough, for we met the Green Knight, the Red Knight, and the Blue Knight, all in quick succession. And the kitchen knight beat them all! I told him he had just been lucky, that their horses had slipped or they had missed their footing. And the annoying thing was that he wouldn't kill any of them, after I had insulted him about the first brother, but he made me ask him to have mercy on them!

"You shall die," he said, "unless this damsel begs me to save your life."

What choice did I have, as a lady is always expected to plead that a life is to be spared? By the time we reached my sister's castle I was heavily in his debt. And to tell the truth, I was beginning to fear for my kitchen knight. He had shown himself to be brave and strong, but he had fought four mighty hand-to-hand battles in as many days, and I knew he had still to face the worse challenge of all — Sir Ironside, the Red Knight of the Red Lands. And what would be the use of bringing my sister a strong champion if he was too exhausted to fight?

We spent the last night of our journey at the castle of the defeated Blue Knight, Sir Persaunte of Inde. He was impressed with my kitchen knight and did him all honor, while I was still calling him "ladle-washer" and "pig-sticker." As always, my hero put up with my insults. That's when I took pity on him and told him that all my unkind words had been intended to spur him on.

"You did what you had to," he said, "and I forgive you. But you should know that I am a gentleman. I am Gareth, the son of King Lot of Orkney, the youngest brother of Sir Gawain and nephew to the king himself. I didn't want anyone at King Arthur's court to know me until I had shown my prowess as a knight."

So my kitchen knight was a king's son, and a worthy member of the Round Table! We had a merry evening after that, and he rose up in the morning

light hearted and ready to face Sir Ironside.

On the way to the castle we passed trees bearing a dreadful fruit — the bodies of about forty knights who had already tried to rescue my sister. They had all been killed and hanged there by Sir Ironside. That was enough to dampen even the courage of Gareth.

When we reached Castle Dangerous, we saw a great ivory horn hanging from a sycamore tree. Then I spotted Lyoness looking out of a high window.

"Look up there!" I said, thinking of a new way to bolster my knight's courage. "That is my sister, the Lady Lyoness. Isn't she beautiful?"

Sir Gareth dismounted, made a deep bow to her and then blew the ivory horn so hard that it broke in two. Out from the castle rode Sir Ironside in his blood-red armor. He and Sir Gareth mounted their horses and ran together with a mighty clash; both their spears broke and their horses fell. The two knights leapt from their horses and fought with swords, hacking off pieces of each other's armor. Their wounds were so terrible that the meadow grass around them was soon red.

The fight went on until evening. When I thought all was lost, Sir Gareth looked up and saw my sister weeping for him at the window. With one last effort he disarmed Sir Ironside and wrenched off his helmet.

"I yield to you, stranger knight," said Sir Ironside.

"You must yield to the lady of the castle," said Sir Gareth, "and give her back her lands. And when we are healed of our wounds, we shall all go back to King Arthur's court."

And so we did. What noble company we had! The Green Knight, the Red Knight, and the Blue Knight were all Sir Gareth's liegemen now, and they brought over a hundred knights with them. Then there was Sir Ironside and his followers. Lyoness and I were dressed in our best attire.

Another surprise awaited us at court. Queen Morgause of Orkney, King Arthur's half sister, had come to visit her sons and was scolding Sir Gawain: "But where is Gareth, your youngest brother, who came to court over a year ago? Where is his place at the Round Table?"

"I am here, mother," said my good kitchen knight, striding up to the king's throne. You may imagine how everyone stared! The kitchen knave in his apron had turned into a handsome knight in armor, followed by a whole train of his own knights. And he had brought with him a beautiful lady with lands of her own.

Sir Gareth and Lady Lyoness were married at Michaelmas, at King Arthur's castle by the sea. It was a splendid wedding with everyone dressed in their finest clothes, and Lyoness was wearing a gold and emerald wreath given to her by Queen Guinevere. At their wedding feast, Gareth teased me about the way I had treated him.

"My liege," he said to the king, "this was the most savage damsel that ever a knight had to serve. Where shall another knight be found to put up with her shrewish ways?"

And I blushed as King Arthur said, "We shall find another knight of the Round Table just as noble-born as you, Sir Gareth, who will tame this savage damsel. What say you, Sir Gaheris?"

Sir Gaheris was one of Gareth's older brothers, and since we had returned to court, we had gotten to know one another very well.

"What say you, Lady Lyonet?" said Sir Gaheris, taking my hand and smiling.

What could I say?

"I must do what my king wishes," I said demurely, and all the court laughed and wished us joy.

But you can be sure that if my heart hadn't turned to Gaheris of its own accord, I should have found a way of getting out of it. I am not known as the savage damsel for nothing!

SISTERS *in* SORCERY:
MORGAN, MORGAUSE, *and* ELAINE

Arthur's half sisters were all married to his former enemies. Morgause was wedded to King Lot of Orkney and had four sons by him who all grew up to be knights of the Round Table. When King Lot was killed by King Pellinore, Morgause took Pellinore's son, Lamorak, as her lover. Her third son, Gaheris, caught her in bed with Lamorak and cut off her head with his sword. The hot-blooded Orkney boys eventually killed Lamorak, too. Morgause's youngest son was Sir Mordred, her child by her own half brother, King Arthur. He was brought up to hate his royal father, encouraged by his aunt, Morgan le Fay. Morgan's story gives us a different view of King Arthur ....

I loathed Arthur from the moment I laid eyes on him. The second sight is stronger in me than in my sisters and as soon as I saw the wailing brat, I knew he was not my father's son. Luckily for him, he was hurried away to a foster family, or I might have smothered him in his crib.

Everyone in Logres was amazed when an unknown young man pulled the sword from the stone! Everyone except me and Merlin. That wily old fox had engineered the whole thing — he disguised the vile King Uther as my beloved father before Gorlois was cold in his grave.

So King Uther had an heir after all! And since he had married my mother, that heir became the next legitimate king. Arthur smirked, and Merlin rubbed his hands. I would have slaughtered them all, just as I had poisoned Uther, but I was forced to bide my time.

My sisters were both married off to kings. They were happy enough. Elaine hasn't the second sight at all, but she's a sweet person, like my father. She lived peacefully with her husband and bore him a son.

As for Morgause, she would have been reasonably happy with any man. It's a pity that her sixth sense didn't warn her what her own son would do to her in the end. Or what would come of sleeping with King Arthur. She didn't know he was our half brother when she invited him into her bed. Anyway, Mordred was the only son Arthur ever fathered — and how he came to regret it! In fact, he regretted it right away, because Merlin came and told Arthur that he had lain with his own sister, and the child to be born the next May Day would be his downfall.

So Arthur ordered all the babies born on May Day to ladies of nobility to be put into a ship and cast adrift at sea. Mordred was one of the unfortunate babes, but when the ship broke up on the rocks near a castle, drowning most of the children, he was rescued and raised to manhood. What a family!

And what of me when my sisters were getting kings and crowns? Well, my mother thought I was too young to be married yet, for I was only a child (though I was not too young to dispose of Uther). She worried about me, knowing as she did that the old magic ran strong in me. So she arranged for me to go into a convent.

I was happy enough with the old nuns. Of course, if they'd known what I could do, and what I had done, and what I would do ... well, they would have crossed themselves and fainted. But I put my years with them to good use. I was a model pupil, though I had no intention of taking the vows.

The convent to me meant one thing — learning. The nuns had a splendid library, much better than the worthless collection of that dumb ox Uther. I studied Greek and Latin diligently, instead of groaning about it like my fellow novices, who preferred tapestry and fine sewing. Every spare minute I had was spent in the library, or in the herb garden with Sister Mary Magdalene, learning the qualities of every plant that grows.

How surprised they all were when I left the convent and went to study with Merlin! This was after I found out that Merlin was the one who had placed King Uther in my mother's bed. It seemed to me that if I were to defeat Arthur, I must learn everything Merlin had to teach. So I studied astronomy, medicine, and prophecy (which the common people call sorcery and witchcraft) with him.

People can be so stupid. Magic is simply knowing how things work. How can you change something if you don't know what makes it the way it is in the first place? I can transform myself into an old hag as ugly as Lady Ragnell or a beautiful young woman as lovely as Guinevere, but only because I know about anatomy and the process of aging.

My time with Merlin wasn't as long as I would have liked because my brother was in a hurry to play matchmaker. He still had one enemy, King Uriens of Gore, and I was the only disposable sister left. So I became Queen of Gore.

I had no objections to being a queen. It gave me a freedom I didn't have as an unmarried girl. Merlin didn't protest at losing his best pupil, because he had just gained a new one — Nimue, the Lady of the Lake.

My husband Uriens meant nothing to me. The best thing Uriens ever did was give me my sweet son Yvain who reminds me of my nephew Gareth. They are both good, gentle knights, with none of the bad qualities of either of their parents. But I never felt any loyalty to Uriens, for I was handed over to him like a piece of furniture.

And when I heard that Uriens had expected to marry Guinevere himself and that Arthur had given me to him as a consolation prize, I felt nothing

but contempt for both of them. I don't hate Queen Guinevere. I'm sorry for her being married to my brother, with no children, and secretly in love with another man. No, she has troubles enough of her own.

I have tried many times to kill Arthur. My first attempt failed because I asked a man to do it. He was my lover, Sir Accolon, as young and handsome as King Uriens was old and wrinkled. Accolon was one of Arthur's knights, and I managed to trick him into fighting his own king.

I thought I had been very clever because I switched the men's swords, so that Accolon had Excalibur and Arthur had the poor substitute. And I stole Excalibur's scabbard, which is even more valuable, and gave it to my lover.

What a fight that was! Both men shed so much blood that it was a wonder they could stand. Arthur suspected witchcraft because he couldn't overcome Accolon with his sword. And then Accolon lifted Excalibur and brought it down on Arthur's sword, breaking it off at the hilt. As Arthur stared at the bloody blade lying in the grass, he realized that it could not have been Excalibur he had held.

"Yield, traitor knight!" cried Sir Accolon, still unaware whose fragile life he held in his hand. And that might have been Arthur's last hour, for he would have fought to the death even with his bare hands. But Nimue, the one people call the Lady of the Lake, had heard about the fight, and made her way to the field. She used her magic to make Accolon drop Excalibur and to put it back in Arthur's hands. There was little doubting the outcome after that.

My plan had been for Accolon to kill Arthur and for me to slay Uriens; then the two of us would have been queen and king of Logres. Everything went wrong. My son Yvain found me with my sword raised over his father and stopped me. But Yvain is not like Gaheris; he wouldn't kill his own mother. He made me promise never to do such a thing again. And he called me such dreadful names that I thought my heart would break.

But that was nothing compared to what I felt when I saw the present Arthur sent me: the body of Sir Accolon. He had died of his wounds four days after their great battle. He had lost too much blood to live. I wept over my love's cold body, white and beautiful as a marble monument. And then I rode off to where Arthur lay sleeping and stole his enchanted scabbard again.

Why should Arthur be protected against all wounds? He has dealt enough of them to other people in his time. So I hurled that hateful scabbard, dripping with its precious jewels, into the deepest part of a lake. It will protect Arthur no longer — unless of course Nimue gets hold of it. Her magic is as great as mine, and she has now chosen to be Arthur's champion.

Nimue thwarted me again the last time I tried to kill Arthur. I sent one of my damsels to Camelot with a rich cloak for the king. It had so many jewels on it you couldn't have squeezed another one in, but they were the result of

my magic rather than of mining.

"My mistress, Queen Morgan, sends you greetings," said the damsel to the king, "and to make amends to you for sending her knight Sir Accolon to fight you, she offers you this fine cloak. Please accept it, with her deepest apologies."

"My thanks to my sister," said King Arthur, pleased with the present. He rose to try on the cloak. But unluckily for me, Nimue was there at court, too. She has always thwarted me!

"Tell the damsel to try on the cloak first," said Nimue.

Every eye in the court was on my poor damsel as she reluctantly slipped her arms into the magic cloak. And every eye in the court saw her burn to ashes, as Arthur would have burned. The king grew very angry and sent my dear son Yvain into exile, believing that he was in conspiracy with me. So now I have a new reason to hate my brother.

It is too dangerous for me to be seen at court now. Arthur has forbidden it. But I am content to bide my time. I have another apt pupil who will help to bring him down — his own son, my nephew Mordred. He feels the same about Arthur as I did about the king's father, old King Uther. And he is very fond of his aunt Morgan since Morgause was killed.

Oh yes, I have great hopes for Mordred. And if he doesn't manage to finish the job, I'll be waiting. I have waited almost all my life to avenge my father's death, and the time is coming ...

The LOATHSOME LADY: RAGNELL'S STORY

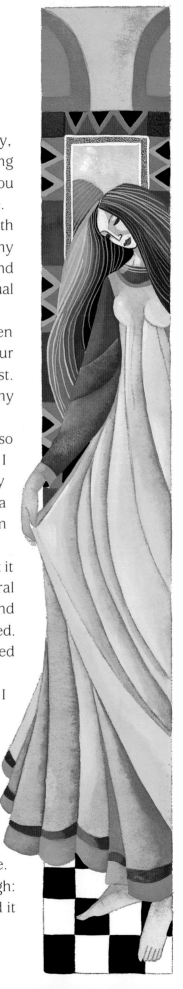

It's easy to be a woman if you are beautiful, but if you are ugly, your life is misery. No matter whether you are kind, loving intelligent, wealthy — if your face and body are hideous, you will be treated as a monster. I know; I speak from experience.

I wasn't born ugly. I can remember looking in a glass with some pleasure when I was little. But that was back in the days when my mother was alive and I was happy. We were a happy family, my mother and father, my older brother Grummer and me, living a life undisturbed by unusual events. I don't think I even knew what magic was.

Then my mother died and everything changed. I was still a little girl when my father remarried. Grummer was older and able to escape from our hated stepmother into boy's pursuits, like learning to ride and hunt and joust. But I, a lonely and miserable little girl, had no opportunity to get out of my stepmother's way.

She hated me. I think she was probably jealous, because my father was so fond of me and often told her how much I resembled my mother. (Now that I am older, I realize that it was not very tactful of him.) She didn't actively mistreat me, never beating me or starving me or making me work like a servant. But she hated me, and her cold glittering eyes followed me from room to room.

I'm not sure when I realized she was a witch. Once I knew, I thought that it was her magic that had ensnared my father. But she had enough natural charms to enchant a man without supernatural help. She was fine-boned and graceful, with long black hair which was always glossy and beautifully arranged. I felt gawky beside her as I grew up tall and graceless, like a ginger-haired peasant beside my elegant stepmother.

And she should have helped me then: God knows I needed a mother as I made the change from girl to woman. But that seemed to make her even more jealous. I have since wondered if it was because she had no child of her own. Her witchcraft couldn't help her there. No matter how many vile-smelling potions she drank or evil-looking lotions she smeared on her body, she remained infertile.

My father didn't mind; he had a healthy heir in Grummer, and he had me. "A handsome son and a beautiful daughter," he would say. "What more could a man want?" and my stepmother would smile her snake's smile.

How did I know she was a witch? Well, in the end I had proof enough: because of her I became the ugliest woman in the kingdom of Logres, and it

was only the courtesy of the finest knight in the land that saved me.

But even as a child, I saw her turn a lazy maid into a rat, watched her transform herself into a night owl and fly from her turret room into the wild woods. And she would use her magic on petty things, like taking Grummer's appetite away as soon as he sat down to meat or unraveling all the cloth I had woven during the day.

She did love my father, of that I am sure, and it was only when he died that she seemed to lose all control. Perhaps she blamed us for his death. But we grieved as deeply as she did. Grummer was old enough to inherit our father's lands, and he took his duties seriously. That brought him into the castle more often, and he noticed how miserable I was.

So he announced that he would give me a handsome dowry and that we would start looking for a suitable husband for me. That was what drove our stepmother to her final madness.

First she cast a spell on the king himself! She made him believe that Sir Grummer — for by now he was a knight — had no valid claim to our father's property. In other words, that he was an illegitimate child. The shame of that would have been bad enough, but King Arthur, believing the rumors our stepmother spread around, took all Sir Grummer's lands away and gave them to his nephew Sir Gawain, but left the castle to her.

Sir Gawain! What a hated name that was to me for so long! Grummer always spoke of him as an unjust tyrant. But soon I had more to distress me than my brother's situation. The day after the king gave Grummer's lands to Sir Gawain, our stepmother came to me to show her pleasure about my misfortune! Grummer, who had come to say goodbye, hid behind a screen as soon as he heard her come in. He couldn't bear to be in the same room with her.

"Where is your dowry now, Maid Ragnell?" said our stepmother. "Your brother has nothing to give you. Yet maybe your pretty looks will still win you a husband. For a man may overlook a woman's poor estate if she carries a handsome enough dowry in her face."

Grummer was listening to every word, and I think he would have burst out and strangled her when he realized what she was about to do, but I motioned to him to stay back. You see, I never believed that one woman would really do to another what she did to me.

She seemed quite crazed as she waved her long white hands over my head and around my body. After muttering some strange-sounding words, she uttered a curse clear enough for us to understand:

"May you stay as loathsome as you are now, by day and by night, until you meet a man willing to let you make your own choice."

She grabbed my mirror and thrust it before my face. I nearly fainted. The creature looking back at me was no longer myself. Its teeth were long and yellow in a hideously wide mouth. The cheeks and nose were fat and ruddy, the eyes bleary like an old man's, the hair matted and unclean. I looked down at my body and found that my breasts had drooped to my waist, which was now as thick as a barrel. My legs were shorter and my shoulders broader than before. There wasn't a part of me that I could look at without horror.

My stepmother shrieked with glee. "There is no man in the world kind enough to let you choose whether to be ugly by day or by night," she hissed. "For if you are ugly by night, you will drive him from your bed, and if you are fair by night for his pleasure, then you will be hideous by day and his pride will never be able to stand the insults and gossip. But that is the choice he must let you make, or you will remain loathsome until your life's end!"

She ran from the room, and I turned to Grummer. He was the first man I saw flinch at the sight of me but not the last — no, not for a long time.

But Grummer's face softened when he saw my tears.

"Ragnell," he said, "forgive me. I know you are still your own true, beautiful self inside. I promise I shall look after you and do everything I can to lift the enchantment. But first I must get my lands back."

Then began the long years of exile. We lived like peasants in a small cottage at the edge of our old estate, given by my father to Grummer's old tutor. This good man gave us shelter, and, when he died, the cottage became my brother's.

I never went outside the cottage; I couldn't bear anyone but my brother to see me. So I never saw Sir Gawain when he came hunting over his land. But I knew whenever he was around, for Grummer became impossible to live with, pacing back and forth and finding fault with my cooking.

I don't know how many years passed in this way, before one hopeful day when Sir Grummer came home in great excitement.

"I have him now!" he proclaimed triumphantly.

"Have who?" I asked.

"The king!" said Grummer. "I have seen King Arthur and got the better of him."

"Oh Grummer, you have not hurt the king!" I said.

"No, not yet," he said, "but I did threaten him. I tricked him away from his companions while he was out hunting, and I ambushed him."

"Grummer, where is he now? Are we not in enough trouble, without your committing treason on the king?"

"I let him go," said Grummer sulkily, "but only on the condition that he give himself up to me in a year's time if he cannot answer a question I put to him."

Grummer wouldn't tell me what the question was, but I vowed to find out. It was wrong for my brother to retrieve his lands by holding the king's life as collateral. So I had to face the world, even though I couldn't face my mirror.

Oh, the cruelty of those months! The vile things that people said to me, the names I was called, the insults that people thought I couldn't hear, as if I were deaf as well as ugly! But it was worth it, because I found out that Arthur was sending messengers throughout the land to help him answer Grummer's question, "What do women most desire?"

What *do* women most desire? Beauty, my heart answered in its agony. Or was it a loving husband, a flock of healthy, pretty children? Someone to love them for the person within? I brooded over the question for many months. And then at last, I remembered my stepmother's words when she enchanted me. Were they the key to undo the spell and restore my brother's fortunes with one stroke?

Sir Gawain had taken on himself the quest for the answer, risking his life to save the king's. Since the land we lived on was now part of Sir Gawain's territories it was difficult not to put myself in his way. But oh, how hard it was to face him looking as I did!

Still, Sir Gawain is a gentleman through and through. Of course his eyes widened and his shoulders stiffened when I crossed his path and called out to him by name. My own brother had reacted similarly. Sir Gawain thought that I was as nature made me. Some of his companions snickered behind their hands, but he courteously asked what he could do for me.

The words came out all wrong from my drooling mouth. "Marry me, Sir Gawain," I slobbered. "For I can give you the answer that will save your life from Sir Grummer Summer Jour."

His followers laughed openly at my jumbling of my brother's name, but Sir Gawain was thoughtful. How handsome he looked, sitting on his tall chestnut horse! His hair and beard were red-gold, his limbs long and straight, his chest broad and muscular, and he had the smile of an angel. If I had been the most beautiful woman in the world, I wouldn't have deserved him and yet, hideous hag that I was, I thought I might trick him into marriage.

Sir Gawain was a bachelor and a young and vigorous one. He would surely jump at the chance to save his life. Maybe he thought I wouldn't live long. After all, I looked about a hundred years old in my bewitched state. But maybe he thought one of the answers he had collected would be the right one and he wouldn't have to marry me at all.

Whatever his reasoning, he said yes.

During the following week the day of reckoning came. Sir Grummer, Sir Gawain, and King Arthur met in the glade where my brother had ambushed the king exactly a year before. None of them knew that I was watching from behind a tree. Sir Gawain formally offered his life instead of the king's, and Grummer accepted the offer.

Then Sir Gawain went through the list of answers he had brought with him.

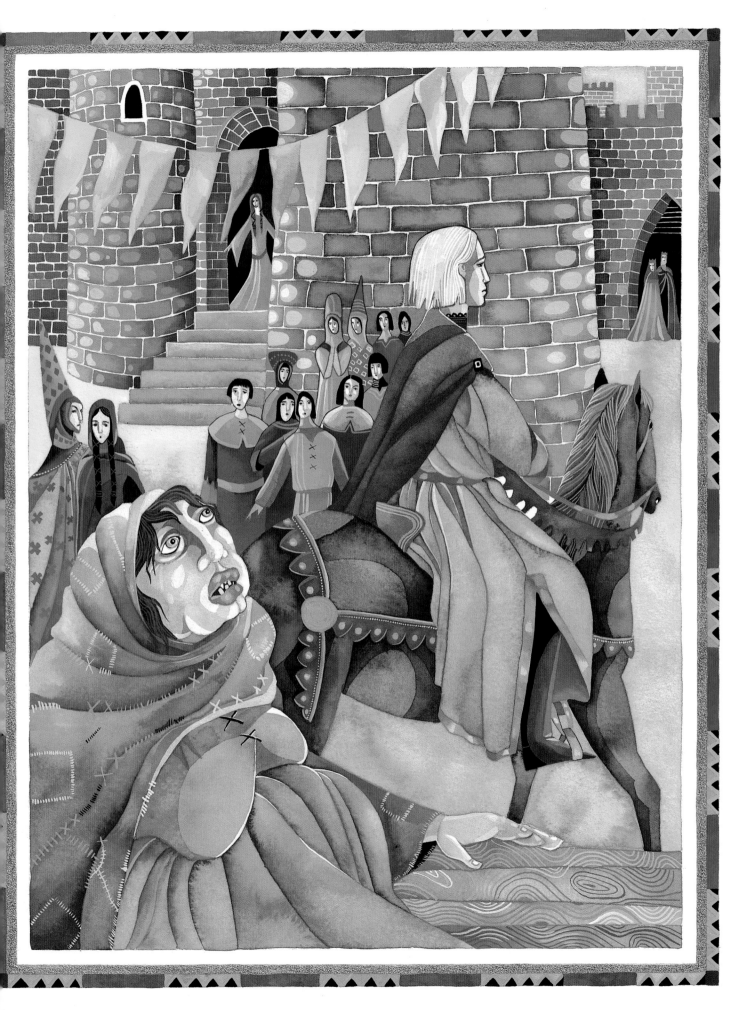

Women, he suggested, want love, beauty, fine dresses, children, husbands, music, perfume, learning, security ...

"No," said Sir Grummer. "No, no, and no. They may want all those things, but none of them is what they most *desire*."

Sir Gawain reached the end of his list. He looked around desperately for some other answer. My heart ached for him as he clutched his forehead and spoke the words I had told him.

"Well then, it must be that what women most desire is their own way, to have a choice about what they do and not to have it decided for them."

The cry of rage from Sir Grummer covered the sound of my deep sigh.

"You must have used witchcraft to know that," said Sir Grummer, "but it is the right answer and, by the rules of chivalry, you and King Arthur are now free."

He turned his horse and galloped away. King Arthur stood for a long time with his arm around Sir Gawain, and I thought I heard my handsome knight weep for joy. I crept miserably back to the cottage ashamed that I had lost my brother's land.

I did not have to wait long for my bridegroom. The dear, honorable man came the same day to claim my hand in marriage and we set out for Camelot. Grummer was furious. He realized what I had done, and he refused to come to my wedding. He thought I was interested only in getting a husband.

Our entry into Camelot was the worst moment of all my bad moments as an ugly woman. Sir Gawain rode with his head held high beside the raised couch that carried me. I tried to hold my head straight, but I know that it lolled on my short neck. I heard the shocked gasps of the ladies of the court and, when I was presented to the king and queen, I saw Guinevere, even the exquisite, high-born Guinevere, suppress a tiny shudder.

It was the queen who suggested our wedding be a private affair, but I was having none of it. I dressed in my favorite scarlet gown and put on the finest of my mother's jewels. This was the ordeal I had to go through to win my good knight. Even worse than the ceremony was the marriage feast. Along with my looks, I had lost my manners and my normal appetite. I know I ate far too much, and disgustingly.

Poor Gawain! His relief at being able to retire to our chamber, out of sight of all the courtiers, soon turned to anguish. This was when I had to summon all my courage, and I think he had to do the same.

"Come to bed, Gawain dear," I croaked in my horrible hoarse voice, "and give your new wife a kiss."

He never hesitated. He even kept his eyes open. And that was how I knew myself transformed back to my proper shape — because I saw the change in his eyes.

"Ragnell," he cried. "Can it be you? You are beautiful!"

"Yes, husband," I said, tears flowing from my eyes. "It is the real me. I have been under an enchantment which you, in your kindness and courtesy, have just broken."

He went to take me in his arms, smiling with delight. But the biggest test of all still lay ahead.

"The enchantment gives me a choice, my dear," I said. "Either I can be like this every night we spend together, but by day I shall be the ugly old woman you saw before. The whole of the court will see me as I was, your hideous wife. Or I can be fair by day and save you from gossip — only then I must be ugly by night, when only you will see me. Which do you choose?"

Gawain sat on the side of the bed with a furrowed brow. At last he turned to me.

"Ragnell, you have suffered such torments from the cruel words thrown at you. I cannot condemn you to endure any more. The choice must be yours."

Oh joy! I flung my arms around him and kissed his dear face all over.

"Then I am free of the spell! And I can be as beautiful as you are pleased to think me all the time!"

Was ever a woman so blessed in a husband? We are now blissfully happy. For as soon as Sir Gawain learned about my stepmother's plot, he gave the lands back to my brother, and King Arthur made sure that the castle was returned to Grummer.

What happened to my stepmother, I do not know. From the day Gawain broke the spell, she was never heard of again.

Castle Adventurous:
Elaine of Corbenic's Story

*One of the most famous members of the Round Table was Sir Lancelot. His skill
and prowess as a fighter were unequaled by any other knight, and his chivalry
was legendary. Lancelot's two great loves, for his king and for Queen Guinevere,
existed side by side for many years, but his split devotion eventually brought
about the downfall of the Round Table. Sir Lancelot was irresistible to women.
Many fell in love with him at first sight. One of them, Elaine, the fair maid of
Astolat, died of unrequited love for him by starving herself to death. Morgan le
Fay tried to tempt Lancelot into loving her on many occasions, but without
success. So she thought of a new way to make him unfaithful
to Guinevere. Her plan involved another Elaine. This is Elaine's story.*

 here was an air of magic about the castle where I was brought
up. It was called Corbenic when I was a girl, but later it became
known as Castle Adventurous. My father, King Pelles, kept a secret
treasure there, greater than any other in all Christendom, and
maybe that was why so many unexplainable things happened
under our roof.

In the hidden chapel stood the Holy Grail, the very cup from which our
Savior drank, the night before his death. It had been handed down to my
father through the centuries from his distant relative Joseph of Arimathea.
The Grail had sacred properties: it could heal souls and bodies, but no one
really understood the full extent of its powers. Even I, who was brought up to
be a handmaid of the Grail, didn't understand it.

But my story begins with a different kind of enchantment. There was
nothing holy about the spells of wicked Queen Morgan of Gore. "Morgan le
Fay" they call her, meaning "the Fairy," for she has powers from beyond this
world that have nothing to do with our Lord.

Neither I nor anyone in the castle could understand why Morgan laid a
cruel spell on me. My torment was to be trapped in a cauldron of boiling
water, like a carrot in a stew. Comical, yes, but agonizing all the same. And
shameful, too, for I was naked as a needle, and had to be rescued by a knight.
And not just any knight, but the best in the land.

Many knights tried to rescue me, but without success. No one had been
able to raise me from the water, kept hot by Morgan's magic, until word of my
suffering reached Sir Lancelot. He came to Corbenic, ready to take up
the challenge, and lifted me out into his arms, proving himself the best knight

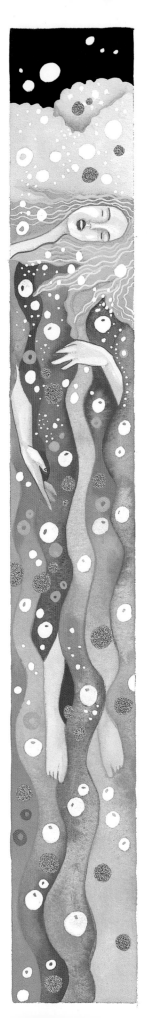

49

in the world. And he proved himself a mortal man, too, for he blushed to hold a naked, dripping young woman in his arms, and quickly handed me to Brusen, my lady-in-waiting, who wrapped me in soft cloth.

I was blushing, as any maiden might, and hoped that it might be understood as my shame at my own nakedness — that, and the boiling water. For I had fallen hopelessly in love. Even if Lancelot hadn't been able to rescue me, I would have loved him from the moment I saw him and been content to boil away in my cauldron for the rest of my life, if only he loved me, too.

But here was the problem: Sir Lancelot du Lac loved no woman but Queen Guinevere, King Arthur's lovely wife. And she loved him, though as a married woman and an anointed queen it was not a love that brought her any honor. Everyone knew about it, except the king himself.

My lady-in-waiting Brusen solved the problem. She told me she would deceive Lancelot into thinking that Queen Guinevere was nearby, and then bring him to me instead. I was far too much in love to protest. So that night, as Lancelot slept at Corbenic, Brusen took a ring to him in his chamber, pretending it was a token from the queen and that she was in Corbenic.

But *I* was the woman in the castle! Brusen led Lancelot to my chamber in the dark, with all the windows shuttered to keep out the light. He suspected nothing until morning, when it was too late. As the sun filtered in through the cracks in the shutters, he leapt out of bed and snatched up his sword.

"Who are you, traitress?" he cried, for he could not see me clearly. But when I told him, he forgave me and put his arms around me and kissed me, so I don't think he minded very much. (People say I was very beautiful when I was younger.)

Lancelot rode back to court, and nine months later I bore him my only child, who was one day to be Sir Galahad, as lovely a son as woman ever held, and of royal blood on both sides.

I missed Lancelot throughout the long years that followed, but I had a daily reminder of him in our son, who looked just like his father. He grew tall and strong with a natural gentleness and grace.

But there was something more about Galahad, which we all sensed from the beginning. He didn't seem like a mortal boy: he was so easy to direct, and never gave me a moment's unease. Except that my motherly heart told me he was not to be long in this world, and I hugged him to me tightly with a love all the fiercer for fear of losing him.

But the time came, many years later, when I could not live another day without a sight of my lord Lancelot. There was to be a great gathering of the court at Camelot, to hold a feast in celebration of King Arthur's recent victories in France. All the lords and ladies of the land were invited, and I told my father that I wanted to go. He had always been in favor of a match between me and

Sir Lancelot, and so he granted permission and said that no expense was to be spared.

I traveled to Camelot with twenty knights and ten ladies, and we all had new overcoats of the richest velvets and brocades, studded with pearls and trimmed with luxurious fur.

As we rode in, I felt the admiring eyes of the whole court on me — all but two. Sir Lancelot du Lac, the only person whose admiration I wanted, turned away at my approach, and it broke my heart. Much later he told me that it was not because he was ashamed of me or our child, but because he remembered drawing his sword on me that morning after Galahad was conceived. That was a deed so disgraceful to his honor as a knight that he couldn't look at me without embarrassment.

I wish I had known it then: we might have both been spared much suffering and pain. But at the time, I could only think that my beloved had snubbed me — and under the cool gaze of Queen Guinevere, his true love. It was more than I could bear. I was presented to the queen and we both smiled and made polite conversation. I could manage it because the blood of kings runs in my veins as well as in hers, but my heart was in turmoil — and so was the queen's.

Brusen was with me, and she suggested playing the same trick on Lancelot as she had done all those years before. It was harder this time, as Guinevere had housed me in a chamber next to hers — a great honor! At the dead of night, Brusen went to Lancelot, saying she had been sent by the queen, and brought him to my bed. No words can tell how good it felt to hold my lord in my arms again.

But our joy was short-lived. Lancelot talks in his sleep, and his voice woke the queen. She stormed in and saw us together.

"False, treacherous knight!" she shrieked. "Leave my court, and do not come to my chamber again! I never want to set eyes on you in this life!"

And Lancelot, realizing what he had done, fainted clean away.

This time there was to be no morning reconciliation between us. When Lancelot came to himself again, he looked back and forth between the queen and me, then ran towards the open window. Just as he was, in his undershirt, he hurled himself out, landed in the rosebushes below, and ran off into the forest, scratched and bleeding.

I turned on Guinevere, not caring that she was my queen and liege lady. "Look what you have done to him!" I cried. "The best knight in the world is now quite out of his wits because of you. And why? Do you not have a lord of your own? And not just a lord, but the first in the land, Arthur, the High King. But that is not enough for you. You had to have my lord, too! For without you, I'm sure that Lancelot would have loved me. And now neither of us shall have

him, for he has gone quite mad!" I did not stay at court long. I cared nothing for Camelot, or the Round Table, if Lancelot had left it. It was two years before I heard anything more of him.

One day, I found a knight sleeping by the fountain in my garden. I recognized him immediately, even though he was as thin as a wild, hungry beast, and his hair and beard were long and matted. But there is no disguising a man like Lancelot du Lac. I had him carried into the castle, still sleeping, and my father and I took him to the Grail Chapel.

There, by the power of its mystery, the Grail miraculously healed my lord of his madness. He woke clear-eyed and in his right mind for the first time since he heard the queen's reproaches. But he didn't know where he was at first, and when everything came back to him, he wept bitterly.

"Alas," he cried. "I have done wrong and can never return to Camelot. King Pelles, let me have a place to live in peace for the remainder of my days."

When I next saw him, bathed and dressed in a red velvet cloak, with his hair and beard cut, he was close to his old self. My father gave him a small castle in which to live on an island called Joyous Isle, and I begged to go and look after him.

Those were our happiest times. Lancelot was quiet and docile and let me tend the wounds he had suffered living wild in the woods for two years. But I could do nothing about the scars on his heart, and I often found him looking out of the window that faced towards Camelot, and the queen.

From that direction two knights came riding one day, who brought to an end my life with Lancelot on Joyous Isle. Sir Ector and Sir Percival were friends and kinsmen of my lord. They had been searching for him for all this time, at the queen's bidding. As soon as he heard the queen's name, Lancelot was blinded by love and returned to Camelot with them.

Our son Galahad was nearly fifteen, and my father said he must soon take his own place at King Arthur's Court. I fought against it, but I knew that he was destined for great things. It was part of the mystery of my father's castle that Galahad's destiny was already known. Besides, the boy wanted to go to Camelot.

So soon after his fifteenth birthday, I sent for my lovely son, dressed him in red silk, and gave him a fur cloak, as befits a descendant of kings. We equipped him with the finest horse and harness and armor, but his grandfather gave him no sword, saying he would find one at Camelot. And we sent him out with a message to Sir Lancelot, saying that none but he should make his son a knight. And we said farewell with many tears, knowing that great things lay before him.

I never saw Galahad or his father again.

The QUEEN'S KNIGHT: GUINEVERE'S LOVE *for* LANCELOT

From the moment the Holy Grail appeared at Camelot, it was the beginning of the end of the Round Table. But cracks were appearing in the fellowship for other reasons ...

When I look back at the foolish girl I was when my father gave the table to King Arthur as part of my dowry, I could weep with pity — for the king, for all the knights who lost their lives in a useless quest and a worse cause, but, most of all, for myself. For the proud queen who believed that those anointed royalty never shed tears!

When did the fellowship start to crumble? Most would say the day that Lancelot came to court. But then again most people blame Lancelot and me for everything that happened. They have no idea what it was like to be the queen of the greatest and most ruthless king who ever lived — a queen who turned out to be an ordinary woman after all, who could find love only outside her marriage.

Lancelot arrived in Camelot just after I lost my third child. By then I was sure that Arthur didn't love me, though the physical passion between us was still strong. I couldn't forgive him for the secret things Morgan had accused him of. I was aching and heartbroken as I received the new knight, Sir Lancelot du Lac, who had come to help Arthur in the war against the Roman Emperor, so I have no clear recollection of our first meeting.

But Lancelot remembers every detail. I was pale as death, he says, but like a lovely ghost. He felt my sorrow enter his bones, and he vowed then and there to be my champion until his life's end. He stayed true to his pledge.

By the time Arthur and his knights returned from Rome, full of their great victory, Lancelot was Arthur's closest friend. The young knight had been bold and fearless in the wars, snatching the Emperor's banner from under his nose in the midst of battle and slaying all he encountered. It was clear that the two men loved each other more than brothers.

Lancelot fell under Arthur's spell like so many young knights before him had. And Arthur was enraptured by his new follower. All through Lancelot's life women, and men, too, have fallen in love with him. (He is beautiful, even now, at the time I write, when we live chastely in separate religious houses. I know if my nuns here at Amesbury had a visit from Lancelot, they would soon forget their vows!) And furthermore, he is the greatest knight in all

Christendom. Only Sir Tristram, Sir Gawain, and Sir Lamorak came anywhere near him in valor and strength — and alas, they are all dead now.

But to return to the years at Camelot. Arthur and Lancelot were inseparable, which meant that Lancelot and I were often thrown into one another's company. I knew that Lancelot had special feelings for me; he was always so protective and gentle, while Arthur treated me as a warrior queen, his equal and fellow general.

I was soon aware how women felt about Lancelot. Even Morgan fell under his spell, though her own spells could never captivate him. He resisted her wiles, and she, with an intuition born more of her womanly nature than her witchcraft, soon found out why. She plagued us throughout the long years of our love.

Once, Morgan sent Arthur a gift of a drinking horn with a note saying that only chaste women could drink out of it without spilling their wine. "Try it on all the ladies of your court, dear brother," her message ended. This was before Arthur realized how much Morgan hated him. But he was far too courteous to apply such a vulgar test to gentlewomen, so he threw the horn away. It was just as well for me: I would have spilled all my wine out of sheer nerves, let alone guilt!

Later, Morgan had a shield painted and sent it to Arthur. It showed a king and queen on a red background. Above them stood a knight, with a foot resting on the head of each crowned ruler. The message was clear enough: Arthur and I were both subject to one of his knights. But my husband chose to ignore the symbolism. He hung the shield in our chamber, where no one could see it but us. I think that was when I first knew that he was aware of how much Lancelot and I meant to each other.

Tongues were already beginning to wag when Lancelot did something that put the rumors to rest for a long time. It pains me still to write about it, although Lancelot has sworn to me a million times that Elaine won him to her by a trick. However she did it, the daughter of the Grail King begot a child by Sir Lancelot, which is more than I have ever done, by either him or Arthur.

Their son was Galahad, who in time became an even greater knight than his father, because his heart and soul were untainted by sin. When I found out about the boy, I nearly went mad. Then Elaine came to Camelot, dressed up in her best clothes, to flaunt her victory over me. How I upbraided Lancelot! But how much worse it was when I discovered he had spent the night with her. For I had summoned him to my own chamber, but when she took the message to him, my waiting-woman found his bed quite empty.

I remember well my anguish when I found them together, and how Lancelot lost his senses and jumped out of the window. He became insane and wandered for two years before he was found again, and then he lived with Elaine on

56

Joyous Isle for some time more before he returned to court.

All the time Lancelot was away, Arthur was miserable, and I was wretched. I swore that if Lancelot ever returned, I would never again drive him away. When he did come back, his son followed soon after and was made a knight of the Round Table. I longed to see the boy, and as soon as I did, I knew that everything I had heard was true. Galahad was his father's son in every line of his face and body. But there was a magical grace about him that reminded me of Arthur as a young man. Galahad was another person men would follow to the ends of the earth.

And Galahad sat in the seat of the Siege Perilous without harm. Those golden letters disappeared and were replaced by his name. But Galahad was in a way even more responsible for the breakup of the Round Table than Lancelot and I. Because while Galahad was at Camelot, the Holy Grail appeared. I didn't see it, but Lancelot told me what happened.

All the knights were seated in their proper places at the Round Table, the full fellowship of a hundred and fifty, waiting for supper to be served. There came a crack of thunder out of a clear sky so loudly that it felt as if the palace would be split in two. And then a beam of light, not lightning but pure radiant sunshine, pierced the hall and all the knights felt filled with grace. They looked at one another like men newly born and spoke not a word.

Then the Holy Grail appeared in the hall. It was covered with white silk and no one carried it: As it moved by itself across the room, it filled the hall with a sweet perfume. Every knight found his plate and goblet overflowing with the food and drink he liked best. But the Grail also filled their hearts with a longing for something more than earthly pleasures and rewards.

And when the Grail departed, the fellowship was left in disarray. All the best knights, including Lancelot and Galahad, set out on the greatest quest the Round Table had ever known. But it was also different from any other adventure: there were no damsels or other people needing help involved. The knights all wanted to follow the Grail wherever it led them, and I knew that the Round Table would never be the same again.

Arthur knew it, too. I sat at my window and watched the models of English chivalry ride out wearing their best armor, and I knew that many of our finest knights would never return.

It was many seasons before the survivors began to straggle back. Galahad had achieved the quest, as anyone might have foreseen, and he became keeper of the Grail. But he died soon afterwards, and Sir Percival, another noble knight, lived not long after him.

Lancelot returned a changed man. Deep lines of grief spoiled his handsome face, but it was not just for the loss of his son. He didn't speak to me for months and when he did it was to say that we must no longer be more than

friends. He had been granted a vision by the Grail, and it told that it was his great sin in loving me that kept him from a fuller knowledge of its mysteries.

Imagine how I felt! Lancelot was my only comfort and joy. Without him, I was a loveless queen in a childless marriage. Arthur's son by Morgause had come to court by then, so often I had to look at the hated face of Sir Mordred and know that he was Arthur's only heir. Morgause had been slain by her son Gaheris for taking a lover. Just as well that Arthur and I had no son to bring me to a similar fate!

I lived chastely with my wedded lord all through the quest for the Grail and long afterwards, too. But in the end, love proved too strong for Lancelot and soon everything blossomed between us as it had before. But then we grew careless.

Having Mordred at court was like bringing a viper to be nurtured in a nest of young doves. Mordred didn't care for Arthur's feelings, nor for his reputation. He wanted the throne for himself and he didn't care how he got it. He enlisted his half brother Aggravaine in his plots.

Soon in open court Aggravaine accused Lancelot and me of adultery and treason to our king. Arthur couldn't ignore that, and we were foolish enough to spend another night together. Lancelot was unarmed and in his nightshirt, alone with me in my chamber, when there was an ambush at the door. Lancelot killed and wounded many knights before he was captured.

I don't blame Arthur for what he did. It is treason for the king's wife to take a lover, and Arthur wept as he gave the order for me to be burned at the stake. I didn't know whether his tears were for me or for the loss of his friend Lancelot. But of course Lancelot wouldn't let me burn. Hadn't he sworn to be my champion until his life's end?

I shivered in my loose dress in the cold courtyard. Arthur was not the only one with tears in his eyes. I knew all the knights, young and old, who stood around me waiting for the pyre to be lit; only a few of them, led astray by Mordred, had ever wished me any harm.

And then Sir Lancelot came. He rode in like a whirlwind, lashing around himself with his sword, not knowing whom he was wounding. Alas, the sword that he used to cut my bonds was stained with the blood of many noble knights. Lancelot wrapped me in his cloak, snatched me up onto his horse and we rode to Joyous Gard.

When we heard the full toll of the massacre at Camelot, we wept in each other's arms. Sir Agglovale and Sir Tor, the brave and hardy brothers of Sir Lamorak and Sir Percival, had both died under Lancelot's sword, and we grieved for them as true knights and true friends. But there was still worse: Gawain's younger brothers Gaheris and Gareth had also been killed — and they hadn't even been armed.

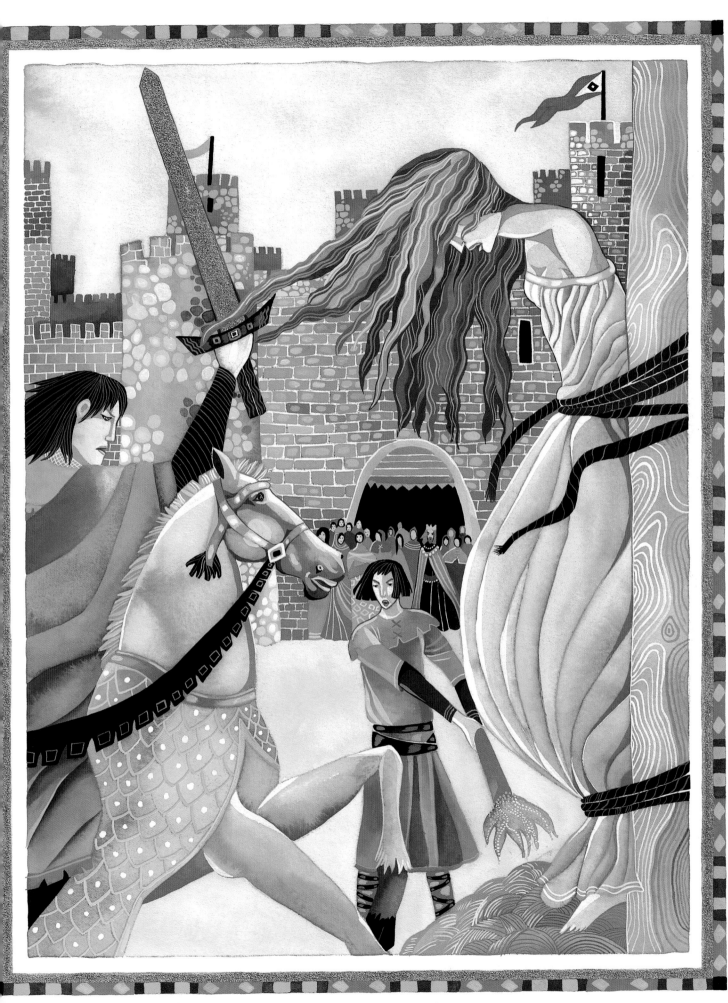

I couldn't mourn for Gaheris, who had killed his own mother, but Gareth! I still remembered him as the gentle boy who had served a year as Arthur's kitchen hand before going off on the quest that earned him his sweet wife Lyoness. Lancelot wept for Gareth as if his heart would break. He remembered knighting him with his own hands, when Gareth's parentage was still unknown.

"Gawain will never forgive me for this," he said. "For I have slain his brothers. And God knows I loved Sir Gareth better than any man, only after Galahad and my lord the king." Later we learned that Arthur had kept the news of Gareth's death from Gawain as long as he could, knowing that Gawain would never rest until he had killed Lancelot and all his kin in revenge.

And the messenger told me that Arthur said, "I am more sorry for the death of these my noble knights than I am for the loss of my queen. For I might win myself queens enough, but never again will be seen such a company of knights as those who sat at the Round Table."

And I knew, though it hurt to hear it, that the messenger spoke the truth.

The ISLE *of* AVALON: THE STORIES' END

When Gawain heard the news of his brothers' death, he swore vengeance on Lancelot. Lancelot was at Joyous Gard with Guinevere, and Gawain persuaded Arthur to besiege them there. For fifteen weeks Guinevere, Lancelot, and his knights were trapped in Joyous Gard. Outside, Arthur and Gawain had mustered a mighty army of knights and nobles from all over Logres.
The Pope in Rome came to hear of it and sent a message that Arthur should take the queen back and make his peace with Sir Lancelot. The king was willing to take back his queen, but Gawain was adamant that since Lancelot was his mortal enemy, Arthur could not take the opposite side of his own nephew.
The glorious company of the Round Table was hastening to its end.
Nimue, the Lady of the Lake, takes up the tale again ...

Ever since my release from Merlin, I have looked after Arthur and his fellowship and protected him from danger. But there was nothing I could do to protect Camelot. Its fate was sealed when my foster son Lancelot first set eyes on Arthur's queen — or perhaps even earlier, when Arthur begot a child by his own sister. Such deeds have their consequences. Scholars like myself may see them written in the stars; we may postpone and deflect them for a while, but in the end the stories must play themselves out.

Arthur took Guinevere back, as the Pope had commanded. With great ceremony and a huge company of knights clad in green velvet, Lancelot and Guinevere, dressed in white and gold — signifying purity and kingly blood — returned to Camelot and the queen was solemnly handed back to her lord. But Gawain, who would never say a word against Guinevere, turned on Lancelot and said, "Get you gone, traitor knight! If you are not out of this kingdom within two weeks, you will forfeit your life." And Arthur could not oppose him, though the tears streamed down his face.

So Lancelot left England and went back to Benwick, in France. For he was now a king in his own right, with great wealth and many lands that he had forsaken all these years to be part of the Round Table. And his followers went with him.

But Sir Gawain was not content merely to send Lancelot into exile. He persuaded Arthur to raise a huge army and cross the channel to besiege Lancelot at Benwick. And Arthur left Mordred in charge of the kingdom, declaring him to be his heir, as both son and nephew, if anything should

happen to him while he was away. He put Guinevere under Mordred's care, and from this came more evil than from her love for my foster son.

Gawain was determined to challenge Lancelot to hand-to-hand battle, and he kept insulting him from outside the wall. "Traitor knight!" he shouted. "False follower of the king and slayer of my brethren! Are you such a coward that you dare not face me?"

In the end, Lancelot could stand it no longer and went out to meet Gawain. It was morning, and he marveled at how Gawain's strength grew with the advancing day. It is true that Gawain had this strange gift, given to him by Merlin, that from nine o'clock in the morning until noon his strength increased with every hour. After that he was his own man again and certainly powerful enough, but for those first three hours he had the strength of three men.

Lancelot did not know about this, and he wondered how it was possible that Gawain grew stronger as he suffered more and more blows. But when noon was past, and Gawain had only his own powers to call upon, Lancelot got the better of him and gave him such serious wounds that any other man would have died of them. But this was not just any man — and three weeks later Gawain was back outside the walls taunting Lancelot. And the same thing happened again.

Life in Logres was perilous for Queen Guinevere, too, with Mordred watching over her in Camelot. She was ready to flee at a moment's warning, for she had never trusted him.

One morning Mordred came to her chamber, bearing letters and an extremely sad face.

"Alas, Madam, all is lost," he said. "Your lord and mine, the gracious King Arthur, is dead. Therefore I must take the throne and rule in his place, and you, my lady, shall be my queen."

Of course Mordred was quite mad. He was Arthur's son, and young enough to be Guinevere's, too. All his life he had been plotting Arthur's downfall. He would make a terrible king. But by then Guinevere was experienced enough in politics to deal with him.

"This is grievous news indeed, my liege," she said calmly. "We must both mourn our private loss, but the kingdom must be served. However, I cannot marry you without some preparations. Grant me leave to travel to London, and there I shall arrange for clothing and festivities for our marriage."

Mordred consented. Wicked as he was, he was not as clever as he thought, letting Guinevere go. She sent messengers ahead to her trusted supporters in London, who provisioned the Tower for a long siege. As soon as she reached London, she withdrew inside the Tower and raised the drawbridge. Mordred was furious when he heard of it. He had himself crowned, but his wedding plans had to wait. For the time being the queen was safe.

I sent word to Arthur of what had happened. Immediately the king returned to England to reclaim his crown and his queen. Gawain came with him, though still half-dead from his two encounters with Lancelot. Lancelot himself stayed behind in Benwick, not knowing why the English army had suddenly left. If only he had known! Lancelot was the one person who might have prevented the tragedy that befell the country and the people he loved.

Mordred's army met the king's forces as soon as they landed at Dover, and there was fierce fighting in the small boats. Sir Gawain suffered a terrible blow that reopened the wound Lancelot had given him in the head. This time Gawain knew he was truly dying, and he asked Arthur to write a letter to Sir Lancelot.

I have that letter in my possession, piteously stained with the great knight's blood: Gawain begs Lancelot to return and rescue both the queen and the kingdom, as he had done so often before. And he asks Lancelot to visit his tomb, for he only has but a few hours to live. Gawain doesn't actually say he forgives Lancelot for the death of Gareth and the others, but the letter refers to the great love that there had always been between the two men. No one could have read that letter and not felt torn with pity for both noble knights.

As soon as noon passed, Sir Gawain died of his old wounds, and King Arthur lamented excessively. Then another blow followed. The people, instead of being pleased to see that their rightful king was still alive, were disappointed. Life under Mordred's short reign had been easy and pleasant because he had been careful not to tax them. All they remembered of Arthur's long years as king was the wars he had waged, and how much they were forced to pay.

The battle at Dover was inconclusive and both sides eventually withdrew to tend their wounded. They intended to fight again, at Camlan. The night before the battle, I sent Arthur a dream in which Gawain came to him attended by the spirits of all the women Gawain had ever defended. "Don't fight tomorrow," he said. "Wait until Lancelot gets here. Otherwise, it will be the worse for you and Mordred."

When Arthur woke, he proposed a treaty with Mordred to postpone the battle for one month. Both armies were already drawn up in their battle lines, while messengers from the two sides negotiated the delay. But Arthur had told his men to watch out for treachery on Mordred's part. He knew what kind of man his son was.

While the talks were going on, one of Mordred's men saw a snake crawl out from a nearby bush and slither toward his foot. The soldier drew his sword to kill the snake and someone on Arthur's side saw the glint of sunlight on the blade. "Treachery!" shouted Arthur's man. "We are betrayed!" And both sides rushed together, with all thoughts of postponing the battle forgotten.

There was never any battle like it in all of Arthur's reign. One hundred thousand men were slain in a single day. Only Sir Bedivere and Sir Lucan were left standing beside the king, and all three men were wounded. Arthur looked out over the bodies lying on the field. On both Mordred's side and his, many noble knights who had once been part of the Round Table lay dead before him.

And then he saw Mordred leaning on his sword, on top of a mound of dead men. With a roar, the king staggered towards him, though his last two knights tried to stop him. "Remember your dream, Sire," they said, "and leave him alone, for you have won the day. After all, there are three of us, and he has no one left standing with him."

But Arthur's blood was hot to avenge his dead knights. He rushed towards his son and thrust his spear into him. Sir Mordred, feeling his death blow, did not resist, but pulled himself further onto the spear and brought his sword down on Arthur's head. It seemed as if they had instantly killed one another, but Arthur managed to crawl back to his last two knights.

Sir Lucan died of his wounds, and Sir Bedivere carried Arthur on his back to the edge of a nearby lake. It was the same lake where I had given the young king his sword Excalibur all those years before. Then Arthur begged Bedivere to throw the sword back into the lake for him. Twice Bedivere was overcome by its worth and beauty and couldn't bring himself to do it. But the third time he hurled it toward the middle of the lake, and I conjured up a silk-sleeved arm to catch it. I was never far from Arthur.

Then I guided my finest barge through the reeds and laid him gently in it. My companions were three queens, a fitting escort for the great king. We took him to the isle of Avalon to be healed.

It is forbidden to tell what happened to him. But one of the queens was Morgan. Make of that what you will. United by magic, we were no longer enemies. After all, we were both taught by Merlin, and Arthur had need of all our skills. It was time for the healing of deeper wounds than those that breach the flesh and let out the warm blood. My years in the Grail Castle have taught me much about reconciliation.

Young Constantine was crowned king, but the people still believe that Arthur will return one day.

Guinevere went into the Abbey at Amesbury and relinquished her green silken gowns for a black and white habit. In time she became Abbess.

And Lancelot? As soon as he received Gawain's letter he set out for Logres with a mighty army, but by the time he got there the battle at Camlan was over, Mordred was dead, and almost every other member of the Round Table, too. And Arthur was missing.

Lancelot turned to Amesbury and the queen as a flower seeks the sun.

But Guinevere was beyond earthly love now. She admitted him to her presence, but spoke before he could say anything.

"Lancelot, you must go back to France. Win for yourself a wife, for I am now intent on saving my soul. It is because of this great love we bore each other that the greatest fellowship of knights there ever was has been broken up and destroyed. And if I see you, I might be tempted again. So I pray you, return to your own kingdom."

"Do you really think I could love any woman after you?" asked Lancelot. "I shall follow your example and enter a religious order. And I shall pray for your soul and the souls of Arthur, Gawain, and the noble knights of the Round Table all the days of my life."

With that, he turned and left. Six years passed and my foster son Lancelot became an ordained priest. So perhaps he will see salvation after all.

But he had one more duty to perform for the queen, his love. When news reached him that Guinevere had died, Sir Lancelot, or Father Lancelot as I must now call him, went to Amesbury with his last few followers. He wept to see the dead queen, particularly when the nuns told him that she had prayed to die before he came to her, for fear she would see his face again and turn her heart away from God.

Lancelot performed her funeral and requiem mass and laid her body in the earth. After that, he never took food or drink again, but spent his days mourning over Guinevere's grave. Within a month he was dead. He had told his kinsmen to take his body back to Joyous Gard, and that is where he now lies.

I still put white roses on his grave every day, and I pray for his soul and Guinevere's. And for King Arthur, the king who was and king who shall be. May their names never be forgotten.

LIST OF CHARACTERS

ACCOLON, SIR Lover of Queen Morgan. He was killed by King Arthur.

AGGRAVAINE Second son of Lot and Morgause.

ARTHUR King of England and head of the fellowship of the Round Table. Son of Uther Pendragon and Igrayne. He married Queen Guinevere. The historical Arthur was a 6th-century chieftain who united the English against the Saxon invaders.

AVALON A mysterious country to which the wounded King Arthur was taken after the battle of Camlan. It is prophesied that one day he will return from there and reign again.

BEDIVERE, SIR One of the last two of King Arthur's knights left alive after the battle of Camlan.

BRUSEN Elaine's waiting-woman, who helped her to entrap Sir Lancelot.

CAMELOT The favorite home of the court of King Arthur. There is no agreement about where it might have been; sites as far apart as Winchester and Scotland have been suggested.

CAMLAN The site of King Arthur's last battle, where he fought against Mordred.

CASTLE ADVENTUROUS The castle of King Pelles, where the Holy Grail was kept.

CASTLE DANGEROUS The castle of Lady Lyoness, besieged by the Red Knight of the Red Lands.

CORBENIC The Grail castle, later known as Castle Adventurous.

ELAINE Half sister of King Arthur. She was married to King Nentres of Garlot.

ELAINE OF CORBENIC Daughter of King Pelles. She fell in love with Sir Lancelot and deceived him into spending a night with her, at which time Galahad was conceived.

EXCALIBUR The sword given to King Arthur by the Lady of the Lake. Its scabbard was woven with spells by the Lady that prevented its wearer from being wounded.

GAHERIS, SIR Son of Lot and Morgause. He married the Lady Lyonet.

GALAHAD, SIR Son of Sir Lancelot and Elaine of Corbenic. He sat in the Siege Perilous without harm, and was the only Knight of the Round Table to be fully successful in the quest for the Holy Grail.

GARETH, SIR Youngest son of Lot and Morgause. After his adventure of the Castle Dangerous, he married Lady Lyoness.

GAWAIN, SIR Eldest son of Lot and Morgause. He married Lady Ragnell.

GORLOIS Duke of Cornwall. Married to Igrayne. He was killed by Uther Pendragon.

GUINEVERE Daughter of King Leodegrance of Camelard. She married King Arthur.

HOLY GRAIL The cup from which Jesus drank at the Last Supper. It was passed down through the family of King Pelles from his ancestor, Joseph of Arimathea. When the Grail left Pelles' castle, it appeared briefly at Camelot, inspiring most of the knights of the Round Table to set off on a quest to find it.

IGRAYNE Duchess of Cornwall. She was married first to Gorlois, by whom she had three daughters, Morgause, Elaine, and Morgan. Later she married Uther Pendragon, by whom she had Arthur.

LADY OF THE LAKE, see NIMUE

LANCELOT DU LAC, SIR Greatest of the Knights of the Round Table until the birth of his own son Galahad. He fascinated many women, but loved only one, Queen Guinevere.

LEODEGRANCE King of Camelard. Father of Guinevere.

LOGRES Former name for England.

LOT King of Orkney. He was married to Arthur's half sister Morgause.

LYONET The savage damsel who came to King Arthur hoping to find a champion for her sister Lyoness.

LYONESS The lady of Castle Dangerous who was besieged by the Red Knight of the Red Lands.

MERLIN Counselor to King Uther Pendragon and later to his son Arthur. A powerful enchanter, he was eventually trapped by Nimue.

MORDRED, SIR The illegitimate son of Arthur by his half sister Morgause. He was brought up to hate his father and plotted his downfall.

MORGAN LE FAY An enchantress, half sister to Arthur, married to Uriens. She schemed to bring about Arthur's downfall most of his life, yet was there at the end to take him to Avalon and heal his wounds.

MORGAUSE Queen of Orkney, married to Lot. She was half sister to Arthur, by whom she had a son, Mordred.

NENTRES King of Garlot. Married to Arthur's half sister Elaine.

NIMUE The Lady of the Lake. A mysterious figure who brought up Sir Lancelot, entrapped Merlin and eventually married King Pelles.

PELLES King of the Grail Castle. Father of Elaine of Corbenic, who later married Nimue.

PERSAUNTE OF INDE, SIR The Blue Knight, defeated by Sir Gareth.

RAGNELL, LADY Sister of Sir Summer Grummer Jour. Caught in a spell, she later married Sir Gawain and was released from the enchantment.

ROUND TABLE Given by Uther Pendragon to King Leodegrance, and later part of Guinevere's dowry.

SUMMER GRUMMER JOUR, SIR Brother of Lady Ragnell.

TINTAGEL The castle of Gorlois, Duke of Cornwall.

URIENS King of Gore. Husband of Morgan Le Fay.

UTHER PENDRAGON King of England and father of King Arthur.

YVAIN Son of Morgan and Uriens. He prevented his mother from killing his father.

ABOUT THE STORIES

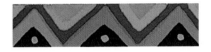

Anyone who chooses to retell the stories of King Arthur runs into an immediate problem. If there was a historical figure who inspired the King Arthur stories, he lived between the end of the 5th and the middle of the 6th century A.D. But almost everything we think we know about him comes from the magnificent English collection called *Le Morte d'Arthur*, written by Sir Thomas Malory in 1485, a thousand years later. Malory based his stories on 13th-century French romances.

I have followed Malory for all the stories (except Ragnell's, which does not appear in *Le Morte d'Arthur*) using *The Works of Sir Thomas Malory*, edited by Eugene Vinaver (Clarendon Press, 1947) and adding information from the following other sources:

IGRAYNE *History of the Kings of Britain*, Geoffrey of Monmouth, published 1136, translated by Lewis Thorpe, (Penguin, 1966).

GUINEVERE *Prose Lancelot from the Vulgate Cycle*, by Geoffrey of Monmouth, published 1210-1230, translated by Corin Corley as *Lancelot of the Lake* (Oxford University Press, World's Classics, 1989); *Guinevere*, Norma Lorre Goodrich (HarperCollins, 1991).

LYONET The story is found only in Malory. He is thought to have found this story in a now lost Anglo-Norman romance.

RAGNELL "The Wedding of Sir Gawain and Dame Ragnell," *Middle English Verse Romances* (edited by Donald B. Sands, University of Exeter Press, 1986). This is a 15th-century English romance and there is also a fragment, "The Marriage of Sir Gawaine," dating from the same time. A version of the story can also be found in Chaucer's "Wife of Bath's Tale" in *The Canterbury Tales*.

MORGAN, MORGAUSE AND ELAINE *Merlin*, Norma Lorre Goodrich (HarperCollins, 1988) has an interesting chapter on Morgan. *Of Arthour and Merlin*, edited by O.D. Macrae-Gibson (Early English Text Society, 1973/1979), based on the 13th-century French prose version of the Merlin story, gives the three sisters' names as Hermesent, Belisent and Blasine. Malory seems to have invented the name Elaine.

NIMUE Goodrich's *Merlin* has a chapter on Nimue, too. She is sometimes known as Vivian(e). I have also used *Of Arthour and Merlin*, by Geoffrey of Monmouth, and the *Prose Lancelot*. Nimue's presence in the last story is mainly my invention, although the detail of her being in the barge with Morgan and the other queens is from Malory.

ELAINE OF CORBENIC This is found only in Malory.

I have added some details of my own, though much of the dialogue is to be found in Malory. If you would like to supplement your reading with a more conventional account which puts the men in the center of the picture, I recommend Geraldine McCaughrean's *King Arthur and the Round Table* (Macdonald, 1996).